Shojo Beat

love★com

Story & Art by
Aya Nakahara

love ★ com

contents 1

HEY!!

KOI-ZUMI!!

AND WITH A LAST NAME LIKE KOIZUMI, WHICH MEANS "LITTLE SPRING"...

RISA, HEY, WAKE UP...

GNOM

WHEEEE

GNMMM

I'VE ALWAYS BEEN TALL FOR MY AGE...

KOI-ZUMI!!

I.E. "BIG SPRING."

IT'S LIKE, "SORRY MY NAME ISN'T ÔIZUMI."

...SO AT SCHOOL ASSEMBLIES AND STUFF I'D ALWAYS BE AT THE VERY BACK.

Shojo Beat

TION KEEP OUT CAU

ON KEEP OUT CAUTI

TION KEEP OUT CAU

Story & Art by
Aya Nakahara

1

SORRY ABOUT THAT.

WHAT'S THE DEAL, YOU UP ALL NIGHT PARTYING OR SOMETHING?

I WAS GAMING ALL NIGHT.

HOW'D YOU EVEN DO IT? TAKES SKILL, SLEEPING ON YOUR FEET.

SORRY.

WHAAAT?! BUT SUMMER VACATION STARTS TOMOR...

ALL RIGHT!

YOUR PENALTY IS TO KEEP COMING TO SCHOOL EVERY DAY!

NOT FOR YOU, IT DOESN'T.

heh heh

YOU'RE WELCOME.

GAMING? AT YOUR COMPUTER? VERY SEXY, KOIZUMI.

Say what?

BEING TALL SUCKS IN EVERY SINGLE WAY.

YOU'VE JUST BEEN ENROLLED IN SUMMER SCHOOL. ATTENDANCE MANDATORY.

YOU STICK OUT LIKE A SORE THUMB ...

WHAAAT?!

SO EVERYTHING YOU DO GETS NOTICED.

HERE YOU GO! ♡

I'M USED TO THAT BY NOW, THOUGH.

AND I GUESS IT IS CONVENIENT FOR REACHING HIGH PLACES.

SNAP

MOVE, JUMBO-GAL!! YOU'RE BLOCKING MY WAY!!

WHUMP

!

YUP.

THIS IS ÔTANI.

"BIG VALLEY," WHEN HE'S REALLY A SHRIMP.

...YOU MAKING FUN OF ME?

YOU BET I AM!!

YOU ASKIN' FOR A FIGHT?! HUH?!

HEY, YOU TWO. YOU "ALL HANSHIN-KYOJIN" THERE!

WATCH IT, MIDGET!!

OH, SORRY, YOU PREFER "BEHE-MOTH," MAYBE?

YEAH. GREAT. THANKS.

THIS THE BOX YOU WANTED?

SOMEONE DOES YOU A FAVOR AND YOU CALL HER JUMBO-GAL?!!

DEE WHAT? A MORE? WHAT?

what's he talking about?!

blah

SAVE THE BICKERING D'AMOUR FOR AFTER SCHOOL.

UGH, THAT WAS IN TOTAL STEREO.

WILL YOU PLEASE STOP CALLING US THAT?!

YOU GUYS'RE GOING OUT WITH EACH OTHER, AREN'T YOU?

NO!!

THE TWO OF US...

5'1"

ATSUSHI ŌTANI

(15)

...ARE KNOWN AS THE "ALL HANSHIN-KYOJIN" OF YEAR 1, CLASS 2.

5'7"

RISA KOIZUMI

(15)

SEE YOU TOMORROW!

Katta Katta

...AND TRIES TO STICK YOU TOGETHER ALL THE TIME.

...EVERY-ONE SEEMS TO THINK IT'S VERY VERY FUNNY...

WHEN YOU HAVE A SUPER-TALL GIRL...

...AND A SUPER-SHORT BOY IN THE SAME CLASS...

AND WHO'D WANNA GO OUT WITH A GIRL WHO SNORES STANDING UP, ANYWAY?

WHY WOULD I EVER GO OUT WITH A GIGANTIC FREAK WHO MAKES ME LOOK EVEN SHORTER THAN I AM?

WE GOT THE "ALL HANSHIN-KYOJIN" MONIKER...

...FROM OUR HOMEROOM TEACHER, MR. YAMADA, WHEN HE PICKED US TO BE THE CLASS REPS.

You guys know "All Hanshin-Kyojin"?

They're this comedy duo, a really tall guy, Kyojin, with this really short guy, Hanshin...

We know them.

We know them.

SO LOUD WE HEARD YOU ALL THE WAY UP FRONT.

I WASN'T SNORING, WAS I?!

NO WAY!

NO, YOU SHOVE OFF!

HEY, SHOVE OFF!

SUBSTI-TUTE "TINY RUNT" FOR "GIGANTIC FREAK" AND YOU GOT MY THOUGHTS EXACTLY.

I DON'T BELIEVE THAT!!

OH MY GOD!

AAAAAGH...

YOU ARE NEVER GONNA FIND A BOYFRIEND.

AAAAAGH...

MWARGH

AAAAARGH! HE PISSES ME OFF!!

LETCHEE? THAT'S REALLY GOOD.

LET-CHEE ABOUT THAT!!

Yeah, letchee! Dope.

OOPS

SORRY, FOLKS, BUT I HAVE NO INTENTION OF FORMING A COMEDY TEAM WITH THIS GUY.

RISA!

YUP, THE VERY ONE! MY GOD, I FAILED 'EM BOTH *BIG*-TIME!

tee hee

Hey!

NO FAIR, I *PASSED* BOTH! WITH A D MINUS, BUT STILL!

YOU MEAN THAT REMEDIAL CLASS FOR PEOPLE WHO FAILED BOTH THE MID-TERM AND THE FINAL?

NO WAY! ME TOO!

I HAVE TO COME TO SUMMER SCHOOL...

For math...

SORRY ABOUT THAT, YOU GUYS.

No biggie.

HOW'D IT GO? WHAT'D HE SAY?

IT MUST BE NICE HAVING STRAIGHT A'S, MUSTN'T IT?

I KNOW, RISA-SAN! COULD SHE BE *MOCKING* US?

GOODNESS! "FOR FUN," SHE SAYS, NOBU-SAN!

STOP IT, YOU GUYS!

IT SURE MUST!

YOU KNOW... JUST FOR FUN...

...UH!

MAYBE I'LL GO TOO... TO THAT CLASS...

The snorer!

IT'S JUST WAY TOO UGLY.

WHAT'S THE POINT OF ATTENDING A UNIFORM-OPTIONAL SCHOOL IF THEY MAKE YOU WEAR IT, ANYWAY?

I hear you.

AT LEAST I'LL GET A BREAK FROM THAT OBNOXIOUS SHRIMP ÔTANI, ANYWAY.

OH, YEAH, NOBU, YAMADA WAS MAD AT YOU TOO.

CUZ YOU WEREN'T WEARING YOUR UNIFORM.

Hey, the snorer!

SO OKAY, I HAVE TO GO TO SCHOOL, BUT STARTING TOMORROW IT'S *SUMMER VACATION.*

YOU KNOW WE'RE JUST KIDDING, CHIHARU! COME ON!

YEAH, BUT I WAS SERIOUS! I DON'T WANNA BE THE ONLY ONE LEFT OUT.

ACTUALLY, I WAS TOTALLY PLANNING TO PLAY HOOKY.

NO, REALLY! I THINK YOU GUYS WOULD WORK!

JEEZ! NOT YOU TOO, CHIHARU!!

NYAAARGH!!

My argh?

I'M NOT EVEN SAYING BOYFRIEND, OKAY? I JUST WISH I HAD A *CRUSH.*

WHAT ABOUT ÔTANI?

THINK THERE MIGHT BE SOME HUNKS?

HEY, IN SUMMER SCHOOL WE'LL BE WITH KIDS FROM OTHER CLASSES, RIGHT?

YOU ALREADY HAVE A BOY-FRIEND.

tee hee ♡

JUST WATCH ME!

I'M MAKING THIS MY SUMMER OF LOVE!!

THAT DOES IT.

IF I DON'T FIND MYSELF A BOYFRIEND SOON...

...I'M GOING TO BE "ALL KYOJIN" FOR THE REST OF MY LIFE.

KLATE

WHAT ARE YOU DOING HERE?!

YOU TOOK THE WORDS RIGHT OUTTA MY MOUTH!

blah

blah

blah

blah

blah

I DID NOT FAIL THOSE TESTS, SO THERE!

THE ONLY REASON I'M HERE IS I GOT CALLED OUT FOR SNORING THROUGH THE END-OF-TERM CEREMONY, ALL RIGHT?!

I'D RATHER FAIL THAN SAW LOGS IN PUBLIC!

THAT SOMETHING TO BE SO PROUD OF?!

LIKE YOU CAN TALK?!

OF COURSE YOU'D BE HERE!

JEEZ, I TOTALLY FORGOT HOW DUMB YOU ARE!

GYAK

THEY'RE PRETTY FUNNY.

HEY, ANYBODY GOT A CAMERA?

I NEVER SEEN 'EM TOGETHER LIKE THAT BEFORE.

HEY, ARE THOSE TWO...

THEY GOTTA BE THE CLASS 2 COMEDIANS!

YEAH—!

KATTA

Darling! Hi!
boy-friend

UH-UH. I'M SITTING NEXT TO NAKAO.

CAN'T STAY AWAY FROM EACH OTHER, CAN YOU?

HEY, IT'S "ALL HANSHIN-KYOJIN"!

I SAT HERE FIRST, ALL RIGHT?

YOU GO SIT FURTHER AWAY.

AT LEAST SIT FURTHER AWAY, WILL YA?

I'M SORRY I'M LATE.

GREAT. TALK ABOUT A ROTTEN START.

WE AREN'T HERE CUZ WE *WANNA* BE!

uh-huh

OH, HEY, SUZUKI.

I HAVEN'T TAKEN ROLL YET, SO I'LL LET YOU GET AWAY WITH IT.

KATA

KATA

OKAY, FROM CLASS 1—

IIDA.

HERE.

UENO.

MIND IF I SIT BEHIND YOU?

HERE.

ŌTANI!! SHUT UP, WILL YOU?!

YOU SIT BEHIND *HER*, YOU WON'T BE ABLE TO SEE THE BLACKBOARD, DUDE.

UH... UM.

NO...

I DON'T.

KTUNK!

heh heh

UH...

SORRY FOR BLOCKING YOUR VIEW...

VREE

I AM IN hasty→ LOVE!!

I BET THAT MEANS HE'S TALLER THAN ME.

Whirl

YOU AREN'T.

I CAN SEE JUST FINE.

...

SNIRK

HERE.

FROM CLASS 5... SUZUKI.

...

SO HE'S IN CLASS 5...

HOME-GIRL. HEY, YO.

I DUNNO.

WHAT'S UP WITH RISA?

Tump

HE IS SO FINE...

GET YOUR BUTT OVER TO EMO BURGER WITH ME.

I GOTTA TALK TO YA.

OOOH, A TOUGH MUNCH-KIN.

CUZ I CAN'T TALK TO YOU ABOUT THIS AT SCHOOL, THAT'S WHY.

HOW COME I STILL GOTTA BE WITH YOU AFTER SCHOOL, DURING SUMMER VACATION?

SHUT YOUR FACE!

DON'T CREEP ME OUT. WHAT?

SUZUKI'S RIGHT UP YOUR ALLEY, HUH?

SO, HEY...

HOT FOR SUZUKI♡

HOW COULD HE TELL?

WH-WH-WHADJA SAY?!

AS IF.

I HAPPEN TO BE A VERY NICE PERSON.

YOU PLANNING TO BLACK-MAIL ME?

I CAN READ YOU LIKE A BOOK.

A COMBO MEAL!

YOU WANT A BURGER?! A FISHWICH?! A COMBO MEAL?!

ALL RIGHT! WHATEVER YOU WANT, IT'S ON ME!

YOU GOT IT!

AND...

REALLY?!! ARE YOU SERIOUS?!

AND THEN DO WHAT I CAN TO GET YOU GUYS TOGETHER. HMM?

IN FACT, I WAS THINKING I COULD MAKE FRIENDS WITH SUZUKI IN CLASS, SEE...

I CERTAINLY AM.

TANAKA.

AND?

AND...

HUH?

OH GOOD! SO HEY, WHADDAYA SAY TO...

...A DAY AT THE POOL?

NO, I DON'T HAVE ANY PLANS...

REALLY?!

Chiharu Tanaka

HM?

WHAT, THIS SUNDAY?

YUP!

YAY! THAT SOUNDS LIKE SO MUCH FUN!

NOBU AND NAKAO ALREADY SAID THEY'RE COMING.

HEY, SUZUKI!

BZzzz

YOU DON'T MIND IF A COUPLE OTHER FRIENDS OF MINE COME TOO, DO YOU...?

Ummmm ...

"ALL HANSHIN" ...?

OH. SORRY.

THE NAME'S ŌTANI!

HUH? NO.

THE MORE THE MERRIER, RIGHT?

SO NOW WE'RE ALL GOING TO THE POOL TOGETHER!!

WANNA BE FRIENDS WITH ME?

UH, OKAY...

AS ALWAYS.

SORRY I'M LATE!

LET'S GET GOING.

It's 360 yen

WELL...

PLUS SHE'S SHORTER THAN ME.

I'D NEVER HAVE GUESSED THAT YOU HAD A CRUSH ON CHIHARU.

BUT STILL...

HE'S RIGHT, CHIHARU IS TOTALLY ADORABLE.

OHHHH.

GUYS TOTALLY SCARE HER.

WHAT ?!

hff

SORRY TO SAY, THOUGH, I HAVE SOME BAD NEWS.

IT WAS LOVE AT FIRST SIGHT, MAN.

WHY NOT, YOU DOPE? SHE'S SUPER-CUTE!

BIG DEAL, SO GUYS SCARE HER!

NOT AFTER SHE GETS TO KNOW *ME*!

OKAY. WHATEVER YOU SAY.

YEAH. LOOK AT HER, SHE'S A WRECK TODAY CUZ OF ALL THE GUYS IN OUR GROUP.

Did you buy your train ticket?

yulp

N-not y-yet

YOU SERIOUS?!

YOU'RE RIGHT! THAT IS SO CUTE!

HEY, YOU...

YEAH!! LET'S DO IT!!

LET'S GO FOR IT!!

YEAH, THEY'RE REALLY GETTING ALONG.

THEY'RE IN A GOOD MOOD.

THE REST IS UP TO YOU, GIRL.

GOOD LUCK TO YOU, TOO!

HE'S LIKE, "WHAT THE HECK AM I DOING HERE?"

YOU GO TALK TO SUZUKI, HURRY.

OH, NO.

I ASKED AND HE SAID HE DOESN'T HAVE A GIRL-FRIEND.

REALLY?!

THANK YOU, ŌTANI!!

THE STAGE IS SET AND I'M GOING FOR IT!

IS IT SO EXCIT-ING?

IT'S JUST WATER...

YES, IT IS!!

A DAY AT THE POOL!!

WOW...

WOOOOOOO!

THIS FEELS SOOO GOOD!

IT'S NOTHING LIKE THE POOL AT SCHOOL!

in shape or size

KA-SPLASH

IT'S BEEN A WHOLE YEAR!!

I KNOW, ME TOO!

LIKE *YOU* CAN TALK?!

WHAT'RE YOU DOING, YOU DOPE?!

YOU TOO!

GO AFTER HIM!

BOM

OUCH!

...

yay yay

YEAH. I WOULDN'T HAVE COME IF I DIDN'T WANT TO.

REALLY?

SORRY...

DID YOU EVEN WANT TO COME TODAY?

OOPS.

GOT CARRIED AWAY AND FORGOT WHAT I'M HERE FOR.

TAK TAK TAK

NO WE ARE NOT!!

ARE YOU AND ŌTANI GOING OUT?

YEAH. PLUS, YOU GUYS REALLY CRACK ME UP.

UM!

OH. OKAY.

WHO GUYS?

OKAY.

WANNA GO SWIM TOGETHER OVER THERE?

SO, IF YOU'RE IN SUMMER SCHOOL, DID YOU FAIL YOUR MATH TESTS?

I MISSED THE FINAL CUZ I WAS SICK.

UH-UH.

OHHH. OKAY.

...

YEAH.

I CAN'T THINK OF A SINGLE THING TO SAY...!

OW!

WHIP

UM...

ANY-THING!

GOTTA SAY SOME-THING!

COME ON!

YEAH?

UH... UMMM...

...

LET'S ALL TOSS THIS BALL AROUND!

SURE, IF YOU WANT.

ÔTANI ...!

PHEW

YOU GUYS HAVING A GOOD TIME?

THAT'S MORE LIKE IT.

WHADJA SAY?!

THAT'S CUZ YOU'RE BEING ALL FAKE AND NICE.

WELL, I DON'T KNOW WHAT TO TALK ABOUT!

LIKE YOU WERE HAVING SO MUCH FUN DOING NOTHING?!

"IF YOU WANT"?! JEEZ!

JUST BE YOURSELF, KOIZUMI. ACT NORMAL!

SHUD

HEY, THAT REALLY HURT!!

OKAY! HERE WE GO!

1.

Hello, nice to meet you! And if we've already met, hello again! Aya Nakahara here.

🐰 nyuweeen

This is already my eleventh book of manga. Wow, that happened fast! "Love☆Com" is apparently short for "Lovely Complex." (hearsay)

I just couldn't come up with a title for this series, so I ended up relying on my editor's wisdom. And since everything seems to get abbreviated these days, we decided to go ahead and abbreviate it for you right from the start.

The ☆ is there like the little paper flag they stick into kids' lunches. That is, it's a sort of decoration. But having to draw it in myself can sometimes be a pain. Love☆Com
↑This is a mistake.

OH...

OH... I DON'T LIKE SCARY STUFF EITHER ...

GYAAA KA-SPLASH!

KYAAAA

NHHH

OOOOOOOH

OH... REALLY ...?

I DON'T REALLY LIKE SCARY STUFF...

bummer

WHAT ABOUT YOU?

WANNA GO ON IT, SUZUKI-KUN?

IT SURE LOOKED LIKE IT!!

THAT WAS SO MUCH FUN!

splash

WE PROMISE TO COME RIGHT BACK!

WOULD YOU GUYS MIND IF WE WENT UP JUST ONE TIME?

SURE...

NO.

...

GULP

...

GLANCE

Hey, no running by the poolside please!

C'MON!

OVER THERE, OVER THERE!!

WHERE DO YOU GO IN?!

...

HEY, DUDES!

WASN'T THAT THE BEST?

IT WAS TOTALLY AWESOME !!

GYAAAGH!

KA-PLOOSH!!

MAN, YOU TWO SURE ARE GETTING ALONG ALL OF A SUDDEN.

WHAT'S UP, YOU GUYS?

WHAAAT ?!

HE, LIKE, DISAPPEARED AS I WAS HEADING OVER HERE TO JOIN EVERYBODY.

WHERE'S SUZUKI?!

OH NO, WE DID IT AGAIN!

THIS IS *YOUR* FAULT!

YO, HERE HE COMES.

WHY'S IT *MY* FAULT?!

WAIT A SEC!

HERE.

THIS OKAY?

I BOUGHT SOME FOR EVERY-BODY.

I GOT THIRSTY, SO I WENT TO GET SOME-THING TO DRINK.

WHERE'D YOU GO?!

Ah!

Yay!

ALL RIGHT, SUZUKI!! THANKS, DUDE!!

YEAH! THANK YOU!

YAY! YOU'LL LOVE IT, PROMISE!

MAYBE I'LL GO ON IT LATER TOO.

ACT NORMAL.

HEY, THIS IS GOING PRETTY GOOD...

IT WASN'T SCARY AT ALL!

THAT WATER SLIDER WAS REALLY FUN.

LOOKS SCARY.

REALLY?

...CHIHARU'S BOY-PHOBIA IS TOTALLY CURED, JUST LIKE HE SAID.

I MEAN...

ŌTANI AND CHIHARU ARE LOOKING PRETTY GOOD TOO.

Look how dark you got.

I know, I tan really fast.

hee hee

HE'S PRETTY AMAZING.

Bye, you guys!

NERVOUS

SHE'LL BE FINE.

YOU THINK CHIHARU'S GOING TO BE OKAY?

I GUESS CHIHARU AND SUZUKI LIVE IN THE SAME DIRECTION.

SUZUKI'S A GOOD GUY.

HEY, THANKS.

FOR SETTING IT UP.

THAT'S RIGHT, YOU GUYS WERE LOOKING GOOD!

AND RIGHT NOW, ALL SHE CAN THINK ABOUT IS ME! ♡

YEAH, SO WERE YOU AND SUZUKI.

GOSH.

YEAH!

SURE!

I SURE HOPE IT WORKS OUT FOR BOTH ÔTANI AND ME.

LET'S KEEP IT UP TOMORROW!

HEY, DUDE. LET'S BOTH MAKE THIS A SUMMER OF LOVE!

...

THAT SUZUKI-KUN'S REALLY NICE, HUH?

LIKE, YESTERDAY HE WALKED ME ALL THE WAY HOME.

HE DID...?

HE'S JUST REALLY CONSIDERATE.

SURE IS.

I DIDN'T MEAN IT LIKE THAT, I SWEAR.

NO, NO! RISA!

NO WAY!!

ARE YOU SAYING WHAT I THINK YOU'RE...

... UH... GOOD.

THAT'S GREAT...

I ALWAYS THOUGHT OF GUYS AS BEING KINDA ROUGH AND ROWDY, BUT...

...SUZUKI-KUN'S REALLY NICE...

HE DOESN'T SCARE ME.

DOESN'T THIS MEAN I'M IN TROUBLE?

Oh!

UH-UH. HE WAS REALLY EASY TO TALK TO.

ÔTANI DOESN'T SCARE YOU EITHER, RIGHT?!

YEAH!

YEAH, BUT YOU GOT ALONG FINE WITH ÔTANI TOO, YESTERDAY.

I MEAN, IF CHIHARU ENDS UP FALLING FOR SUZUKI TOO...

I DON'T STAND A CHANCE ...

...ÔTANI ...

YOU'RE IN BIG TROUBLE, DUDE...

I THINK IT'S BECAUSE HE'S SO SMALL. I DON'T EVEN THINK OF HIM AS A GUY.

... MORNING.

WORGH!

MY GOD, IF HE HEARD THAT...

GOOD MORNING, TANAKA-SAN.

YESTERDAY WAS VERY NICE, WASN'T IT?

tee hee

YOU ARE SO FUNNY, ÔTANI-KUN!

HI, ÔTANI-KUN.

Ô... ÔTANI...

MORNING!

I'M KOTANI.

SHAKE

PLEASE TELL THE TEACHER THAT KOTANI WILL MISS CLASS TODAY. KOTANI IS...

COME BACK, ÔTANI, COME BACK!!

SHAKE

MY NAME IS NOT ÔTANI.

IT'S KOTANI, BECAUSE I'M SMALL.

What was that sound?

ÔTANI...

DASH

KOTA-NIIIIIIII!!

KO...

IT'S ÔTANI.

KOTANI...

OOPS

ÔTANI!!

YOU'LL BE OKAY, ÔTANI!!

GO AHEAD, YOU GUYS. I'M GOING AFTER KOTANI!

ÔTANI!

IT'S ÔTANI.

hanh

...I TOLD YOU, IT'S KÔTANI, ALL RIGHT?

NOW WHAT?

...

HEY! DON'T GIVE ME ATTITUDE WHEN I'M JUST TRYING TO SHOW SOME CONCERN!!

MAYBE I'M A LITTLE UPSET!!

GRRRR

WHAT? YOU GONNA GIVE ME A PEP TALK?

WHAT DO I SAY?

UMMM...

KA-POW

YOU MEAT-HEAD!!

SO SHE SAID YOU'RE SMALL, BIG DEAL!

BE A MAN ABOUT IT!

SHE'S SAYING I'M *NOT* A MAN *BECAUSE* I'M SMALL!!

AND THEN A GIRL YOU LIKE SAYS IT ONE SINGLE TIME AND YOU'RE LIKE, SCARRED FOR LIFE?!

LOOK, YOU'VE BEEN CALLED SMALL AT LEAST A THOUSAND TIMES!

BIG OR SMALL, TALL OR SHORT, YOU GOT A �incomprehensible, YOU'RE A GUY!!

WHO CARES?!

HEY, GIRLS AREN'T SUPPOSED TO USE THAT KINDA LANGUAGE!!

SCUM!

...DON'T EVER FALL IN LOVE AGAIN!

THAT'S PATHETIC! WELL, IF THAT'S WHAT YOU'RE LIKE...

JUST WHEN I WAS STARTING TO THINK HE MIGHT BE OKAY AFTER ALL.

...YOU HIT ME RIGHT WHERE IT HURTS JUMBO GAL.

AAARGH, I SWEAR! THAT REALLY PISSES ME OFF!!

STUFF LIKE THAT JUST REALLY GETS ME!!

...

WELL, FORGET HIM!

I'M GONNA GO FOR IT ALL BY MYSELF, THEN!

THAT STUPID SHRIMP.

I THOUGHT HE SAID HE WAS GOING FOR IT.

MORNING.

Oh.

SUZUKI-KUN.

OOPS.

SORRY AB...

WHUMP

CAN'T GET UP IN WINTER, EITHER.

I CAN'T GET UP IN SUMMER.

WEREN'T YOU LATE THE FIRST DAY, TOO?

...OH...

OH...

...UM, I THINK CLASS HAS STARTED ALREADY...

YEAH. I'M LATE.

OH!

GOOD. ME TOO.

HEY, THANKS FOR ASKING ME ALONG YESTER-DAY.

I HAD A GREAT TIME.

ARE YOU LATE TOO?

UH, NO, I JUST... ER...

Um...

TANAKA-SAN SEEMED KINDA SCARED OF ME YESTERDAY.

HEH?

...UMM—

AM I SCARY?

YEAH?

SHE'S SCARED OF GUYS IN GENERAL.

SO I DON'T THINK IT'S YOU IN PARTICULAR.

"THAT SUZUKI-KUN'S REALLY NICE, HUH?"

OKAY...

OH...

THAT'S RIGHT.

WHAT WOULD HAPPEN IF I GOT HIM?

JUST WHAT IF!

WHAT IF...

...AND SHE JUST HASN'T NOTICED IT YET.

MAYBE CHIHARU HAS A LITTLE CRUSH ON HIM...

YEAH.

UH... OH, REALLY?

huh?

I'M NO GOOD AT TALKING TO GIRLS, EITHER.

I THINK IT'S PROBABLY BECAUSE OUR EYES ARE AT ABOUT THE SAME HEIGHT, SO I DON'T FEEL LIKE I'M TALKING TO A GIRL.

WHAT IF I GET HIM?!

Shna

BUT...

WITH YOU, IT'S KINDA...

LO TEK LOTEKHOLOGY

DIFFERENT...

DA-DOON

OH...

I HEARD SOMETHING A LOT LIKE THAT JUST A LITTLE WHILE AGO.

AHHH...

OKAY...

SLUMP

HUH?

EXCUSE ME?

WHAT IF? YEAH, *RIGHT.*

WHAT A DOPE.

SO IT'S NOT LIKE TANAKA-SAN HAS A PROBLEM WITH *ME* IN PARTICULAR.

HMM...

RIGHT...

...HUH?

WELL. I...

...BETTER GET TO CLASS.

I DON'T, OKAY?

...

NO, OF COURSE NOT.

UH-UH.

D-DON'T TELL ME Y-YOU HAVE A CRUSH ON CHIHARU, SUZUKI...

WHAT DID YOU JUST SAY ??

IT'S HOT OUT.

I'M JUST HOT.

NUH-UH.

BUT YOU'RE BLUSH—

IT'S TOTALLY OBVIOUS!

HE TOTALLY HAS A CRUSH ON HER!

NO WAY. I DON'T BELIEVE THIS.

HEY, YOU. ÔIZUMI.

ÔTANI...

LOOK AT YOU, ALL CRUMPLED IN A HEAP AFTER YELLING AT OTHER PEOPLE AND CALLING THEM PATHETIC.

IT *DOES* REALLY GET YOU DOWN...

WHAT'S UP WITH THAT?!

...SORRY. I TAKE ALL THAT STUFF BACK. FORGET I EVER SAID IT.

EVEN IF YOU THINK YOU'RE USED TO IT, MOST OF THE TIME...

IT REALLY HURTS WHEN THE GUY YOU LIKE SAYS IT...

hypo-crite!

Burrrain'

32

I DON'T EVEN ...

A JUMBO-GAL LIKE ME DOESN'T EVEN COUNT...

MIGHT'VE KNOWN SUZUKI WOULD PREFER A CUTE, TINY GIRL...

I can't believe you socked me!!

mwa ha ha ha

HEY, THAT HURT!!

KA-POW

YOU MEAT-HEAD!!

PAY-BACK TIME, SO THERE!

32

ŌTANI...

I'M STILL GOING AFTER HER!

I'M NOT GIVING UP ON CHIHARU, YOU GOT THAT?!

GOOD, SO YOU REMEMBERED WHAT YOU SAID.

THOSE WERE MY GRANDPA'S DYING WORDS...

snif

I'M THE ONE WHO SAID THAT!!

WAIT A MINUTE!

I MEAN, I HAVEN'T EVEN DONE ANYTHING YET.

...DON'T EVER FALL IN LOVE AGAIN!"

"IF YOU'RE GONNA BE SCARRED FOR LIFE OVER SOMETHING LIKE THIS...

HEY, I'M REALLY GLAD I HAD YOU AROUND TODAY.

ÔTANI ...

CUZ IF I DIDN'T, I'D HAVE JUST STAYED REALLY BUMMED OUT.

BUT WE BOTH HAVE THE SAME COMPLEX: OUR HEIGHT.

OUR PROBLEMS ARE THE EXACT OPPOSITE...

BUT I PROBABLY UNDERSTAND HIS FEELINGS BETTER THAN ANYONE ELSE.

THIS GUY REALLY PISSES ME OFF SOMETIMES.

SO WHEN ÔTANI SAYS HE'S GOING TO GO FOR IT...

...IT MAKES ME FEEL LIKE I CAN, TOO.

YEAH.

AND I'M GONNA GO AFTER SUZUKI!

THANKS FOR YELLING AT ME, ÔTANI.

LET'S GO FOR IT!!

SMAK

CUZ IF I GIVE UP NOW ...

...I'LL END UP HUNCHED OVER, ALWAYS WORRIED ABOUT MY HEIGHT.

KATTA

SORRY FOR BEING LATE!

WE WERE WORKING ON NEW MATERIAL FOR OUR ACT.

LATE? THE CLASS IS HALF OVER, YOU GUYS.

Huh? Hi

ha ha ha

WELL, AT LEAST YOU GOT A DECENT EXCUSE.

OKAY, OKAY.

Really.

I DON'T.

LO TEK

WE WERE DOING SLAPSTICK.

YOUR FACE LOOKS KINDA RED AND SWOLLEN, ŌTANI-KUN.

You okay?

SO, LADIES AND GENTLEMEN ...WHERE IS THE STORY OF THIS LOPSIDED DUO GOING TO LEAD?

FRESH MILK
100% ☆

NOT MY SUMMON MONSTERS TOO!!

POP

ARGH!!

TODAY, I'M STARTING OVER AND GOING AFTER SUZUKI AGAIN.

CHAPTER 2

SO, TO KEEP MY MIND OFF OF THAT STUFF, I STAYED UP ALL NIGHT GAMING.

"SO IT'S NOT LIKE TANAKA-SAN HAS A PROBLEM WITH ME IN PARTICULAR."

"I THINK IT'S PROBABLY BECAUSE OUR EYES ARE AT ABOUT THE SAME HEIGHT, SO I DON'T FEEL LIKE I'M TALKING TO A GIRL."

I CAN'T LET STUFF LIKE THAT GET TO ME.

WERE YOU JUST GAMING IN YOUR SLEEP?

UH...

I'M JUST GOING TO FORGET ALL ABOUT IT.

I HAVE TO ADMIT...

...MY HEIGHT IS NOTHING COMPARED TO MY TOTAL LACK OF SEX APPEAL.

HEH HEH...

WELL.

WHAT AM I SUPPOSED TO DO? HOW SHOULD I GO AFTER HIM?

A SECRET MEETING?

BZZZZ

HUH? WHERE'D RISA GO?

and took off.

SHE SAID SHE HAD SOME SECRET MEETING WITH ŌTANI.

I SWEAR, I CANNOT BELIEVE WHAT A GIANT DORK YOU ARE.

I MEAN, IF ON TOP OF BEING HUGE, YOU HAVE NOTHING GOING FOR YOU...

THERE'S NO WAY SUZUKI'S GONNA FALL FOR YA.

I see it even in my dreams...

I GOT KINDA OBSESSED WITH BEATING THE LAST BOSS, SEE...

...USE IT TO MAKE YOUR-SELF HOT!

YOU GOT TIME TO OBSESS OVER YOUR GAMING ...

YESSIR ...

ÔTANI...

"I DON'T EVEN THINK OF HIM AS A GUY."

RELAX.

BELIEVE ME, I KNOW HOW YOU'RE FEELING SO WELL IT HURTS.

HEY! DON'T PUSH IT, KIDDO! YOU EVER HEARD OF DIPLOMATIC LANGUAGE?

LOOK, THIS IS YOUR PARDNER HERE JUST GIVING YOU SOME HONEST ADVICE, OKAY?

JUST LEAVE ME ALONE!!

SO YOU CAN DO "NORI-TSUKKOMI." GREAT, WE'LL ADD IT TO OUR REPERTORY.

Ho!

HEY, YOU PICKIN' A FIGHT WITH ME, BEAN-POLE?!

DRINK IT UP, KID. LET'S BUILD THAT DINKY, UNDER-SIZED BODY OF YOURS SO IT AT LEAST STARTS TO RESEMBLE A MAN'S!

HERE, TAKE MY MILK.

YOU BEING TALL AND ME BEING SHORT ARE OUTSIDE OUR CONTROL.

WHAT THAT MEANS IS, WE GOTTA WORK ON THE OTHER STUFF.

I'm keeping your milk.

...

SO, ANYWAY.

THANKS, I WILL. I'LL DO MY BEST TO GROW ...

THIS IS KIND OF WEIRD.

I KNOW THAT.

OMIGOD!! THAT'S RIGHT, I WON'T HAVE CLASS WITH HIM ANYMORE!

YOU WIMPING OUT ALREADY?

LISTEN, SUMMER SCHOOL'S GONNA BE OVER IN A WEEK, ALL RIGHT?

AND NOW HERE WE ARE GOING HOME TOGETHER AND HAVING THESE STRATEGY SESSIONS...

I MEAN, I THOUGHT OF ÔTANI AS A TOTAL PAIN.

I'M RUNNING OUT OF TIME!

CUZ ME AND TANAKA ARE IN THE SAME CLASS ALL YEAR.

I GOT THE EDGE OVER YOU THERE.

Yipes

HEY, DON'T PANIC.

I DON'T KNOW... YOU THINK?

IF WE REALLY HUSTLE, WE STILL HAVE A CHANCE.

IT'S NOT LIKE THOSE TWO ALREADY GOT TOGETHER OR ANYTHING.

SURE. IF YOU DO THE SAME WITH TANAKA.

REALLY?!

PUSH COMES TO SHOVE, I CAN CALL HIM AND WE CAN DO STUFF TOGETHER.

COOL! AND I'LL PLUG YOU TO SUZUKI, TOO!

TOTALLY! I'LL TELL HER WHAT A GREAT GUY YOU ARE AND STUFF!

IF THIS HADN'T HAPPENED ...

I WOULDN'T EVEN HAVE NOTICED WHAT A NICE GUY ŌTANI IS.

YEAH! BYE!

GO, ME! GO, ŌTANI!

SO I'LL SEE YOU TOMORROW!

THAT ŌTANI! WHAT A GUY!

SERIOUSLY, ŌTANI'S A GREAT GUY!

I MEAN, IF ŌTANI DOESN'T GET CHIHARU...

...SHE'LL END UP GETTING TOGETHER WITH MY SUZUKI.

YEAH. I'M TELLING YOU, YOU COULDN'T FIND A BETTER GUY ANYWHERE!

UH-HUH... THAT'S GREAT.

WOW, RISA'S TOTALLY CRAZY ABOUT ŌTANI.

I SWEAR, ŌTANI'S THE BEST!!

AND HE'S SUPER-NICE, TOO!

...

SURE HE'S SMALL, BUT HE'S GOT GUTS!

THERE! THAT OUGHTA DO IT. ♡

UH-HUH.

WOW, ŌTANI'S TOTALLY CRAZY ABOUT KOIZUMI.

KOIZUMI ROCKS, MAN!

ÔTANI—!

Wohhh

Bzzzz

NAKANO JUST SHOVED THIS MEGA-CHORE AT ME. I SWEAR...

WHAT?

HE THINKS THE CLASS REPS ARE HIS PERSONAL SERVANTS. NOT TO MENTION, IT'S SUMMER VACATION.

WHAAAAAT?!

HE'S IN THE GYM.

HE HAS BASKET-BALL PRACTICE TODAY.

HEY, NOBU. YOU SEEN ÔTANI?

Buoi see ya.

HEY, RISA. YOU WANT ME TO HELP OUT TOO?

OH, YEAH. NAKAO PLAYS BASKET-BALL, TOO.

I WAS GONNA WAIT FOR MY DARLIN' TO GET OUT OF PRACTICE, ANYWAY.

YOU WILL?!

YOU WANT ME TO HELP YOU OUT?

OH.

HEY, SUZUKI-KUN. CAN YOU HELP US OUT, TOO?

THANK YOU SO MUCH, YOU GUYS. I LOVE YOU!

IF YOU GOT THE TIME.

HUH?

Me?

NICE GOING, NOBU!!

OKAY, SUZUKI-KUN. COULD YOU DO THESE?

TUMP

UH. YEAH.

IT SURE IS.

Hot again today, isn't it...

...Hey, Suzuki-kun...

OH, NO.

Here.

Can I have the stapler?

I'LL BE FINE, NOBU, REALLY...

WAA-ARGH!

OH, GO ON.

WAIT... UM...

WHAT ?!

THANKS. HEY, SUZUKI-KUN, COULD YOU GO WITH HER?

WILL YOU?

YOU WANT ME TO GO OUT AND GET US SOME SNACKS?

I'M HUNGRY.

klattan

DON'T YOU THINK THOSE TWO SEEM TO LIKE EACH OTHER?

HEY.

Aaaah...

Aaaaah...

I'LL GO TOO!

I MEAN, COME ON. HE'S NUTS ABOUT HER, THAT'S FOR SURE.

YOU WHAAAT ?!

...ME AND MY DARLIN' DECIDED WE'RE GONNA HELP THEM GET TOGETHER.

BUT THEY'RE BOTH SO SHY AND ALL, SO...

YOU...

YOU STAY HERE AND WORK.

BAM

batta batta

LIKE, DUH. IT'S ONLY TOTALLY OBVIOUS.

...YOU THINK...?

...

...

YOU HELP THEM OUT TOO, RISA!

SO!

YEAH... I GUESS...

AND SHE KINDA SEEMS TO LIKE HIM, TOO.

BZZZZZ

...GOING FOR IT IS JUST A WASTE OF TIME...

...MAYBE...

Why me, of all people...

mutter

WHAT?

UH, NOTHING.

FWEE

SKREE

SKREE

CHECK HIM OUT, HE'S REALLY GOOD!

HEY, THERE'S ŌTANI!

Hey!

ARE YOU GUYS ALL WAITING 'TIL WE'RE DONE?

HEH?

MAYBE ANOTHER TEN MINUTES.

HOW MUCH LONGER?

BWMM

SKWEE

BWMM

SKWEE

SHE'S RIGHT.

YOU WOULDN'T THINK SUCH A SHRIMP COULD PLAY BASKET-BALL...

WHOA, FAST MOVE...

BUT WOW, HE REALLY IS PRETTY GOOD.

SKWEE

HEY, ÔTANI!!

FWEE-FWEEEE

SLDH

WOW!

AMAZING JUMP...

BWUM!

ALL YOU WERE GONNA DO IS GET INTERCEPTED!

HUH...

THAT COACH IS BEING SO TOUGH ON HIM.

POOR GUY'S GETTING YELLED AT AGAIN.

...SORRY...

WHAT'RE YOU DOING?! YOU THINK YOU'RE GONNA SCORE FROM THERE, YOU HALF-PINT?!

BOW

YES-SIR...

THE GUY'S TOTALLY CHEWING HIM OUT.

BET HE MAKES VARSITY NEXT YEAR.

I KNOW, BUT THAT'S CUZ ÔTANI'S REALLY GOOD.

...YESSIR...

PASS THE BALL, KID, PASS THE BALL!!

67

HEY, RELAX, HE'S ALWAYS LIKE THAT.

...THAT DUDE'S REALLY STARTING TO PISS ME OFF.

THINK ABOUT YOUR HEIGHT BEFORE YOU GO JUMPING, SHORTY!!

GRRRR

Thanks, sir.

ALL RIGHT, KIDS, THAT'S ENOUGH FOR TODAY!

KLAP

...YESSIR.

Argh, why doesn't our school have showers, man?!

Gawd, I'm thirsty.

All Kyojin and her wonderful friends

WHAT THE HECK ARE YOU GUYS ALL DOING THERE?!

DARN IT!

TANAKA'S GOING HOME WITH SUZUKI AGAIN.

YOU GOTTA GRAB HIM FIRST, YOU DOPE!

...

...THAT KINDA THREW ME.

I NEVER SAW ÔTANI LOOK LIKE THAT BEFORE...

...

"MIDGET!"

"OOOH, A TOUGH MUNCHKIN."

KOI-ZUMI!

HEY, KOIZUMI! I'M TALKING TO YOU! HEY!

"HERE, TAKE MY MILK. LET'S BUILD THAT DINKY, UNDERSIZED BODY OF YOURS."

Bye you guys!

You're creeping me out here...

I just got goose bumps...

I'M SORRY. I FEEL REALLY BAD...

...FOR ALWAYS CALLING YOU A SHRIMP AND STUFF.

...I'M SO SORRY, ŌTANI...

HUH?

WELL, I DIDN'T REALIZE, SEE...

OH. YEAH. WELL, YOU SEE, AS IT HAPPENS...

WE WERE TALKING ABOUT WHY SUZUKI AND TANAKA ARE GOING HOME TOGETHER WHEN YOU WERE RIGHT THERE!

LOOK, WHO CARES ABOUT THAT NOW?!

I KNOW, RIGHT?

THAT SHOT HE STOPPED ME IN THE MIDDLE OF, IT DEFINITELY WOULD'VE GONE IN!

THAT COACH OF YOURS REALLY TICKS ME OFF!

CALLING YOU "SHORTY" AND ALL THOSE NAMES!

TANAKA SAW ME GETTING BAWLED OUT BY THE COACH TODAY, DIDN'T SHE?

...OH, DARN IT.

"YOU BEING TALL AND ME BEING SHORT ARE OUTSIDE OUR CONTROL."

"WHAT THAT MEANS IS, WE GOTTA WORK ON THE OTHER STUFF."

MAKE HIM THANK THE DAY HE WAS LUCKY ENOUGH TO HAVE ME ON HIS TEAM!

JUST YOU WAIT. I'M GONNA SHOW HIM.

SO I'M SHORT. I MAKE UP FOR IT BY JUMPING HIGHER, MAN.

I THOUGHT YOU WERE REALLY COOL.

SAYS WHO?

GOSH DARN IT, THOUGH. WISH TANAKA HADN'T SEEN THAT.

TALK ABOUT PATHETIC ...

YOU WERE TOTALLY COOL.

YOU REALLY WERE.

AND WHAT'S SO COOL ABOUT GETTING YELLED AT, ANYWAY...

WHAT'S WITH YOU TODAY...

I'M SERIOUS!

YEAH.

blush

blush

COOL.

...UH...

YEAH?

"HE'S NUTS ABOUT HER, THAT'S FOR SURE."

OH... UM.

YEAH.

GOOD LUCK? FOR WHAT?

GOING AFTER SUZUKI, YOU DOPE! SUZUKI?

Hello?

WELL, HEY! GOOD LUCK TO YOU TOO!

SMAK

OW!

WHAAT?!

I CAN'T...

NAKAO AND NOBU'RE TRYING TO GET THOSE TWO TOGETHER.

SURE, BUT BETTER MAKE IT JUST THE FOUR OF US.

NOT WHEN HE TAKES ALL OF THAT COACH'S FLAK AND KEEPS FIGHTING.

I CAN'T SAY STUFF LIKE "GOING FOR IT'S JUST A WASTE OF TIME" TO HIM.

OH, YEAH. THAT'S RIGHT.

NAKAO SAID THE SUMMER FESTIVAL'S COMING UP SOON.

YOU WANNA GO, ALL OF US TOGETHER?!

I BET ÔTANI'S HEIGHT BOTHERS HIM A LOT MORE THAN MINE EVER BOTHERED ME.

OKAY, SO I'LL ASK TANAKA TO COME.

GOT IT.

AND YOU ASK SUZUKI, GOT IT?

YEAH, BETTER SEPA-RATE WHEN WE GET THERE.

ha ha ha

AND THIS TIME, LET'S TRY TO STAY FOCUSED. NOT LIKE THAT DAY AT THE POOL.

I BET HE'S GONE THROUGH A LOT MORE PAIN BECAUSE OF IT THAN I EVER DID.

AT LEAST THAT'S HOW IT SEEMED TO ME TODAY.

BUT I WAS WRONG.

...I KNEW HOW ÔTANI FEELS BETTER THAN ANYONE ELSE.

I THOUGHT...

BUT THAT'S OKAY.

I GUESS I DIDN'T UNDERSTAND ÔTANI'S FEELINGS AT ALL.

TOMORROW? SURE, OKAY.

OH, AND...

ÔTANI'S COMING TOO.

OH, GOOD!

SO WHICH ONE...

Wow, haven't been to a festival in a while.

They're gonna have fireworks!

...DOES CHIHARU LIKE BETTER?

OH DEAR...

SO IS CHIHARU.

OH. UH-HUH.

76

ŌTANI'S GIVING IT ALL HE'S GOT.

OH. OKAY.

GLOOM

I LET IT DOWN AS FAR AS IT WOULD GO.

I CAN'T MAKE IT ANY LONGER THAN THAT.

...ISN'T THIS TOO SHORT?

MOM ?

DARN IT.

JEEZ, MOM, IT'S NOT LIKE I'M GROWING ON PURPOSE, YOU KNOW.

HOW LONG DO YOU PLAN TO KEEP ON GROWING?

EVERY SINGLE YEAR, I HAVE TO TAKE OUT THE HEM.

It wears me out.

TMP TMP

77

I THOUGHT I'D GO "FEMININE" WITH THIS YUKATA...

...AND ALL IT DID WAS EMPHASIZE HOW BIG I AM.

ÔTANI!

KLUNK

KLUNK

I KNEW IT!!

NO...

I LOOK FUNNY?! IS THIS JUST WEIRD?!

I SHOULDN'T HAVE WORN THIS!!

I DIDN'T RECOGNIZE YOU...

YOU SCARED ME...

WHAT?!

Hey, wake up

CHIHARU AND SUZUKI AREN'T HERE YET?

2.

I am incredibly slow at coming up with story lines, which is a big problem. The preview cuts in *Bessatsu Margaret* have to be drawn months ahead, when nothing's been decided yet, so I generally end up lying big-time. This month's was a real whopper. There's a point when a lie gets so big you have to call it fraud. It's unbelievable. Oh!! If any of you have old copies of *Bessatsu Margaret*, please don't ever go back and look at those previews...

oh man...

Not that this has anything to do with anything, but I had never bought *Bessatsu Margaret* until I debuted as an artist... I'd always been a *Deluxe Margaret* reader. And I read *The Margaret*, too. Buying a copy every month can be pretty hard work... Oh! But please do!! There's lots of way better manga than this one inside!
......? Hey, don't put yourself down like that...
Come on, gotta go for it...
Okay, I'll try harder from now on...

OH, GOSH. I THINK I WANNA GO HOME...

I HAVEN'T SAID ANYTHING YET.

WELL, GOOD, DON'T!!

CUZ I DON'T WANNA HEAR IT!!

...HFFF...

YOU WERE LAUGHING AT ME!! I HEARD YOU!! YOU WERE!!

SORRY TO KEEP YOU WAITING, YOU GUYS.

I WASN'T, THAT WAS...

WE BUMPED INTO EACH OTHER... ON THE WAY OVER HERE...

...THIS WAY.

HUH?

shwawawawawa

WHUMP

OH. EXCUSE ME.

BVH

BVH

BVH

BVH

Impressed

HE SWITCHED SIDES WITH HER SO SHE WOULDN'T HAVE PEOPLE BUMPING INTO HER ANYMORE.

BUT ALSO PRETTY DARN SLICK!

THAT WAS PRETTY CRYPTIC!

YEAH.

OH...

YOU'RE RIGHT.

NERVOUS

AWKWARD

ACTUALLY, THEY LOOK LIKE THEY'RE ALREADY TOGETHER, BUT IT'S THEIR FIRST DATE.

THOSE TWO'RE LOOKING REALLY GOOD, LIKE, IT'S JUST A MATTER OF TIME.

...SO NOW WHAT?

WHADDAYA MEAN?

I COULDN'T GET IN THERE IN A MILLION YEARS.

LOOK AT THEM.

...IT'S HOPELESS, AFTER ALL.

HM?

THERE'S NO POINT GOING AFTER HIM.

FORGET ABOUT SUZUKI.

WHAT?

I QUIT.

...ÔTANI.

AND WHO WANTS TO BUST IN AND GET IN THEIR WAY WHEN THOSE TWO'RE LOOKING SO GOOD?!

THERE'S NO WAY I'M GONNA GET HIM.

BUT...

...KOIZUMI...

THAT'S IT.

I'M GIVING UP ON HIM.

...YOU KNOW...

TANAKA?

WHENEVER SHE'S TALKING TO ME, SHE KEEPS GLANCING OVER AT SUZUKI ALL THE TIME.

NOT THAT HE WAS EVER INTERESTED IN ME IN THE FIRST PLACE.

KOIZUMI.

WHAT?

HUH...

PRETTY DARN RUDE, HUH?

YUP.

REALLY?

THAT OKAY WITH YOU?

MAYBE WE OUGHTA JUST LEAVE THOSE TWO ALONE TOGETHER.

DON'T WANNA BUST IN AND GET IN THEIR WAY.

WE DIDN'T DO TOO GREAT WHEN WE WERE *ON* STAGE, THOUGH!

ha ha

THAT WAS QUICK.

"OKAY, WE'RE OUTTA HERE! THANK YOU VERY MUCH!!"

COMEDIANS GOTTA KNOW WHEN TO LEAVE THE STAGE!

YEAH. FACT, I WISH THEY'D HURRY UP AND GET TOGETHER!

YOU SURE?

MAKE ME FEEL A LOT BETTER!

LET'S FORGET ABOUT THOSE TWO AND GO HAVE A GOOD TIME!

ALL RIGHT!

YEAH!

THANK YOU, ÔTANI.

8.

I'm writing this at the beginning of February... and my nail, which split right down the middle on New Year's Eve, with half of it falling off, has finally grown back.

. . . .

Oh my!! What is wrong with this person?! Is she trying to gross us out with this awful, painful-sounding story?!

Speaking of painful stories, once when I was working at a bakery, I was slicing bread with the slicing machine when my finger...

Gyaaaaaaagh!!

What am I, stupid?! It's starting to hurt just from writing about it!! Gyaaaaaagh!!

Oh man...

Be very careful with your fingers, please.

...HUH?

TIP

TIP

TOE

RISA...?

ÔTANI-KUN...?

I'M JUST SO GLAD...

...THAT I HAVE ÔTANI HERE WITH ME.

blah

blah

blah

NOODLES

CHOCOLATE

CHOCOLATE

ED ICE

CORN

CUZ IF I'D BEEN ALONE, I THINK I'D HAVE GOTTEN REALLY DEPRESSED.

Goldfish Scoop

Goldfish Scoop

TAKOYAKI

LET'S START OUT SCOOPING GOLDFISH!

YEAH, YEAH!

YAY!

WOW!

LOOK AT ALL THE STANDS!

Ya dope!

SHOOT FOR PRIZES

SHOOT FOR PRIZES

THE GUY I LIKE IS WITH SOMEONE ELSE, BUT I'M HAVING A GOOD TIME.

THIS IS SO FUN!

IT'S BECAUSE ÔTANI'S WITH ME.

ha ha!

I KNOW, HUH?

IT'S LIKE, WHAT DID WE COME HERE FOR AGAIN?

YEAH. DON'T YOU?

YOU THINK THE OTHER TWO WENT HOME ALREADY?

...HE'S RIGHT.

WHAT DID WE COME HERE FOR?

I MEAN, WHO SPENDS HOURS AND HOURS AT FESTIVAL STALLS EXCEPT LITTLE KIDS AND US?

ÔTANI ...!!

I'M RIGHT HERE, YA DOPE.

...HUH?

ÔTANI ...?

FWI FWIP

OOH!

HEY ÔTANI, LET'S DO THAT ONE NEXT...

TURTLES TURTLE

IT TOTALLY THROWS ME OFF, OKAY?

DON'T DO THAT, IT'S FREAKY.

I THOUGHT I LOST YOU.

YOU PICKING A FIGHT?

YOU'RE SO LITTLE IT'S HARD TO SEE YOU.

GRRIP

LET'S GO GET SOMETHING TO EAT, C'MON—

OH. SORRY.

...HIS HANDS ARE TOTALLY A GUY'S HANDS.

HE'S SHRIMPY, BUT...

ALL KINDA BONY...

WHADJA SAY?!

YOU KNOW, YOU'RE SHRIMPY, BUT...

NOTHING...

HE'D KILL ME IF I SAID THAT TO HIM.

so I won't.

WHAT IS THIS?

Klak

Scoop CASTELLA

psst

YOU THINK THOSE TWO ARE A COUPLE?

PROBABLY. I MEAN, THEY'RE HOLDING HANDS AND EVERYTHING.

giggle

BUT THE GUY'S WAY SHORTER THAN THE GIRL.

so cute!

THIS IS THROWING *ME* WAY OFF, OKAY?

DROP

OOPS.

...IT'S CUZ YOU'RE SO SMALL.

...

GREAT, WE GOT LAUGHED AT CUZ YOU'RE SO TALL.

WHAT ABOUT YOU?

...NAH. WASN'T REALLY HUNGRY.

DIDN'T YOU WANNA EAT?

...UH...

ACTUALLY, I ATE AT HOME BEFORE I LEFT.

blah

blah

blah

CHOCOLATE BANANAS

GUESS YOU'RE RIGHT.

blah

blah

blah

...WHAT IS THIS?

IT'S...

IT FEELS WEIRD.

...

WANNA GO HOME?

...KINDA WEIRD ...

THAT ONE ON TV?

with the funny jingle.

BIG SALAD WITH KOREAN DRESSING.

WHADJA HAVE?

YEAH, THAT ONE.

the guy with the perm.

...YEAH.

...WAS IT GOOD?

...

...HUH.

...

...YEAH.

...

HEH?

RISA, I'M SO SORRY!

BUT WE'RE THE ONES WHO DIS-APPEARED ON YOU...

NO, THAT'S NOT WHAT I MEANT!

WHAT'S SHE TALKING ABOUT?

UM... I THINK THERE'S BEEN SOME KIND OF MISUNDER...

AND GUESS WHAT?!

SUZUKI-KUN TOLD ME...

...THAT ÔTANI'S TOTALLY CRAZY ABOUT YOU, TOO!!

NEXT TIME I WON'T COME ALONG, OKAY? EVEN IF YOU ASK ME!

HUNH ?!

OKAY?!

YOU SHOULD JUST GO WITH ÔTANI!

HUH ...?!

SUZUKI-KUN AND I WERE TOTALLY IN YOUR WAY, WEREN'T WE?!

I KNOW THAT YOU'RE TOTALLY CRAZY ABOUT ÔTANI AND STUFF, SO I SHOULDN'T EVEN HAVE TAGGED ALONG!

I DON'T KNOW.

HOW DID *THAT* HAPPEN...?!

NEXT THING I KNOW, SHE'S WISHING ME GOOD LUCK!

GOOD LUCK FOR *WHAT?!*

WHAAT?

ME? ABOUT YOU?

LOOK, JUST SO YOU KNOW...

THERE IS NO WAY I COULD EVER FALL FOR A JUMBO-GAL LIKE YOU, OKAY?

...I DON'T KNOW.

NO WAY!! NOT IN LIKE, A MILLION YEARS!!

I KNOW THAT.

...HEY...

UH...

I KNOW THAT, OKAY?

WELL, GOOD, CUZ I SURE DON'T WANT A MIDGET LIKE YOU!!

LOVELY COMPLEX

...THE SUMMER OF LOVE I'D BEEN HOPING TO HAVE...

SO ANYWAY...

...ENDED BEFORE IT EVEN STARTED.

blah

PASS YOUR SUMMER HOME-WORK UP TO THE FRONT, PLEASE.

blah

AND IF YOU DIDN'T DO IT, STEP UP TO MY DESK AND COME CLEAN.

ha ha ha

CHAPTER 3

MIGHT'VE KNOWN IT WOULD BE YOU TWO.

BEFORE I KNEW IT, THE REST OF VACATION WAS OVER AND SCHOOL HAD STARTED AGAIN.

TUMP

SO...

SO DON'T LUMP ME TOGETHER WITH THIS GOOF-OFF!

I *DID* MY HOMEWORK, OKAY?! I ONLY FORGOT TO BRING IT, THAT'S ALL!

WHAT DO YOU MEAN, "MIGHT'VE KNOWN"?

HEY, YOU GUYS! HEARD YOU SPENT THE SUMMER WORKING ON YOUR ACT!

FWEE

HA HA HA HA HA

I WOULD'VE *DONE* THE HOMEWORK IF I'D REMEMBERED WE *HAD* ANY!

WHO SAYS I'M A GOOF-OFF?!

ha ha ha

I *KNEW* THEY'D START GOING OUT.

woo hoo ha ha ha

AMONG OTHER THINGS! WHAT'D THEY DO THE REST OF THE TIME?

I DID NOT!

IT'S BETTER THAN COPYING NAKAO'S HOMEWORK AND THEN FORGETTING TO BRING IT IN!

THAT'S EVEN WORSE, YOU BONE-HEAD!

100

WE'RE TALKING ABOUT THE FACT THAT YOU TWO FINALLY GOT TOGETHER THIS SUMMER.

EXCUSE ME?!

WAIT A...

...MINUTE! WHAT'RE YOU GUYS ALL TALKING ABOUT?!

smirk

OH, COME ON, WHO DO YOU THINK YOU'RE FOOLING?

EVERYONE KNOWS YOU WERE AT THE SUMMER FESTIVAL TOGETHER, HOLDING HANDS AND EVERYTHING. WE ALL SAW YOU!

AND SO...

...BEFORE WE KNEW IT...

...Ôtani AND I HAD GONE BEYOND COMEDY DUO TO BECOMING OFFICIALLY RECOGNIZED SWEETHEARTS OF YEAR 1, CLASS 2—

YUP! I SAW YOU GUYS THERE!

I SAW YOU TOO! ♡

I DON'T LIKE HIM!!

I'M SO SURE! YOU COULD'VE TOLD US YOU LIKED ÔTANI INSTEAD OF PRETENDING YOU DIDN'T ALL THE TIME!

—BUT HEY...

NOBODY ASKED US!!

BUT WHAT?

BUT YOU WERE HOLDING HANDS WITH HIM, RIGHT?

OH, REALLY...

I DON'T LIKE HIM!!

NO! WELL, YES, BUT!!

THAT WEIRD FEELING THAT NIGHT...

...Right.

...I WAS BUMMED OUT ABOUT GIVING UP ON SUZUKI.

...WAS PROBABLY JUST BECAUSE...

I AM...

...NOT GOING OUT WITH HIM!!

ŌTANI LOOKED GOOD TO ME BECAUSE HE HAPPENED TO BE THERE.

BECAUSE HE HAPPENED TO BE THERE!!

IT COULD'VE BEEN ANYBODY!!

I OUGHTA SUE YOU FOR OBSTRUCTING TRAFFIC HERE.

YOU'RE SO BIG IT'S A PUBLIC NUISANCE.

OH, EXCUSE ME, I DIDN'T SEE YOU CUZ YOU'RE SO TINY... SHRIMP.

...

MOVE, JUMBO-GAL.

JUST LOOK AT THEM...

I AM GOING TO KILL YOU, I SWEAR!!

THEY SHOULD USE YOU IN NANO-TECHNO-LOGY! AS A HUMAN NANOBOT!

SHUT UP, MICRO-BOY!!

WHAT'D YOU CALL ME?!

CHIHARU ...?

SO HOW COME...

hft

hft

hft

...

Just like us, huh?

THEY CAN'T STAY AWAY FROM EACH OTHER.

YEAH, I KNOW.

GREE

LUCKY DUCKS...

MOVE!

WHUMP

OW!

HEY, THAT REALLY HURT!!

PEGASUS

hft

hft

PEGA

I HAVE TO GO TOO, RISA. I HAVE PREP CLASS TODAY.

BYE, RISA— WE'RE GOING. SEE YOU TOMORROW!

OKAY. SEE YOU GUYS.

"THERE IS NO WAY I COULD EVER FALL FOR A JUMBO-GAL LIKE YOU, OKAY?"

HOW COME...

...THAT MAKES ME SO MAD?

OH, WAIT. YOU KNOW WHERE ŌTANI WENT?

NO PRACTICE TODAY, BUT HE'S SHOOTING HOOPS ON HIS OWN.

HE'S IN THE GYM.

...

CUZ WE HAVE A GAME COMING UP.

...HUH.

ARGH!!

UM, HI. EXCUSE ME?

GRRR

WHAT?!

STILL, WHO SAYS HE GETS TO SKIP CLEANING THE CLASSROOM? IT'S HIS TURN TOO.

SORRY TO BOTHER YOU...

UH...

...WELL, UH...

SO... HOW CAN I HELP YOU?

NO, NO, NO, NO! I'M SORRY ABOUT THAT!

SCRAMBLE

SUZUKI!

I CAN COME BACK IF YOU'RE IN A BAD MOOD...

tee hee

WHAT...

...IS *THIS* ABOUT ...?

Thank you very much.

DO YOU HAVE A LITTLE TIME AFTER YOU'RE DONE HERE?

PEGASUS

I GOT SOME FREE TICKETS TO A MOVIE.

YOU WANNA GO SEE IT TOGETHER?

NO... I'M NOT DOING ANYTHING THIS SUNDAY...

HUH?!

...SO, HEY. ARE YOU DOING ANY-THING THIS SUNDAY?

IS HE GOING TO ASK ME QUESTIONS ABOUT CHIHARU?

EH?!

Da-doom

WHO, ME?!

YEAH.

DA-DOOM

DA-DOOM

HANG ON...

...JUST ONE SECOND!

DA-DOOM

SURE, I...

NO, I...

WHO, ME?!

YOU CAN'T...?

YOU MEAN *ME?!*

YEAH.

MAYBE IT ISN'T HOPE-LESS AFTER ALL...!!

I MEAN, I TOTALLY GAVE UP ON SUZUKI...

MAYBE I SHOULDN'T HAVE?! I STILL HAVE A CHANCE?!

BUT THERE'S FOUR OF THEM...

THE MOVIE TICKETS.

WHAT'RE THESE...?

HMM...?

...like maybe Chiharu...?

...

I THOUGHT YOU MIGHT WANT TO ASK ŌTANI TO COME.

AND MAYBE...

...ONE OF YOUR OTHER FRIENDS.

OKAY, SO MAYBE I'LL ASK NOBU TO COME INSTEAD.

ANY ONE OF YOUR FRIENDS, REALLY!

UH-UH!

WHY GO TO ALL THIS TROUBLE, THOUGH?

WHY NOT ASK HER STRAIGHT OUT, AND GO TO THE MOVIE WITH JUST HER?

SO YOU DO HAVE A CRUSH ON CHIHARU, HUH? I JUST KNEW...

JUST KIDDING.

I DON'T!

...

AND I CAN'T TALK EITHER.

...

SEE, TANAKA-SAN...

SHE WON'T TALK TO ME AT ALL IF IT'S JUST THE TWO OF US.

I DON'T KNOW ABOUT THAT.

SO I DON'T THINK SHE'D EVEN COME IF I ASKED HER TO A MOVIE.

TRY REALLY HARD, HMM...?

YEAH. IF YOU TRY REALLY HARD TO TALK TO HER, I BET SHE'D TALK TO YOU.

YOU THINK?

SO I DON'T THINK YOU HAVE TO TAKE IT PERSONALLY, YOU KNOW?

I TOLD YOU BEFORE, CHIHARU NEVER COULD TALK TO GUYS, FROM WAY BACK.

FINE, WHATEVER.

SWIP

YOU TOTALLY DO HAVE A CRUSH ON CHIHA—

OH, COME ON.

I DON'T!!

I SWEAR

OKAY...

I'LL ASK CHIHARU TO THE MOVIE.

OH...

OKAY...

YOU CAN PAY ME BACK BY TREATING ME TODAY.

SURE. I WAS GONNA ANYWAY.

...PFFFT.

YAY!

SILLY ME.

GOT ALL EXCITED FOR NOTHING.

SO I'LL CALL YOU!

YEAH.

I AM SUCH AN IDIOT.

THAT WAS A WASTE OF TIME...

THAT AN INDIRECT WAY OF CALLING ME A SHRIMP?

YOU WANT ME TO BE DIRECT ABOUT IT, I CAN BE.

WHAT, I LOOK LIKE A MUGGER TO YOU?

YOU ARE OUTSIDE MY FIELD OF VISION, OKAY?!

SO DON'T JUST POP OUT AT ME LIKE THAT!!

HEY.

FWA

GYARGH!!

WRONG!!

SUZUKI—

I DIDN'T ASK HIM TO SEE ME, OKAY?!

I HAVEN'T SAID ANYTHING YET.

Y-YOU WERE WATCHING THAT JUST NOW?

I SAW IT.

...

...SUZUKI.

SEE WHAT...?

MM-HMM... I SEE...

...

THAT'S...

...NOT EVEN...

BUT YOU AREN'T OVER HIM YET, ARE YOU?

YOU SAID YOU WERE GONNA FORGET ABOUT SUZUKI...

WHAT'S THAT MEAN...?

...WELL, MAYBE...

YOU'RE RIGHT...

I ONLY DECIDED TO BACK OFF OF TANAKA CUZ YOU SAID THAT.

YOU'RE THE ONE WHO SAID WE SHOULDN'T BUST IN AND GET IN THEIR WAY.

YOU BIG TRAITOR—

SO ACTUALLY YOU STILL HAVE A CRUSH... ON HER...?

NO WAY, DOPEY. I'M NOT A WISHY-WASHY LOSER LIKE YOU.

WHEN I SAY I'M OUTTA THERE, I'M OUTTA THERE. I'M A REAL MANLY KINDA GUY, ALL RIGHT?

REALLY?

YEAH.

SO I'M THE ONLY WISHY-WASHY LOSER AROUND HERE.

THAT SOMETHING PEOPLE SAY ABOUT THEMSELVES?

A MANLY KINDA GUY ...?

I GOTTA, CUZ NOBODY ELSE SAYS IT.

JEEZ, I'M HOPELESS.

ALL TALK, NO WALK.

I COULD'VE TOLD YOU THAT WAY BACK.

OKAY, WE'VE COME THIS FAR, LET'S MAKE SURE THOSE TWO GET TOGETHER.

THAT'LL MAKE IT EASIER FOR YOU, RIGHT?

YOU WANT ME TO SOCK YOU ONE TO HELP YOU DECIDE?!

SO WHICH IS IT?! YOU GIVING UP ON HIM OR NOT?!

WAPGH!

No way Jose!

WAY TO GO!

I'M GIVING UP ON HIM. I ALREADY HAVE!

SO IS HE NICE, OR IS HE A JERK?

IT SEEMS LIKE...

YEAH...

...ÔTANI'S ALWAYS COMING TO MY RESCUE.

HE'S HARD TO FIGURE OUT.

FINE. I'LL HELP YOU OUT, THEN.

NO! I DON'T KNOW WHERE YOU GOT THAT.

WOULDN'T YOU RATHER GO WITH JUST ŌTANI?

BUT...

A MOVIE?

I'M NOT GOING OUT WITH ŌTANI, OKAY? AND I DON'T HAVE A CRUSH ON HIM, EITHER!

THE FOUR OF US?

YUP!

SUZUKI-KUN WILL BE THERE TOO, RIGHT?

UM... WELL, UH...

IS THAT FOR REAL?

IT'S TOTALLY FOR REAL.

MURF

GRR

...

WHAT'S THE MATTER, CHIHARU?

OH. OKAY...

plop

plop

plop

WHEN I'M WITH HIM, I GET SO NERVOUS...

...THAT I CAN'T THINK OF ANYTHING TO SAY!

...I CAN'T TALK TO HIM.

WH-WH-WHAT'S THE MATTER, CHIHARU?!

WHAAAT?!!

fluster

fluster

HUH?!

CHIHARU...

OH, NOTHING!

DON'T WORRY, CHIHARU. I'LL TAKE CARE OF THIS FOR YOU!

YOU WIN, I LOSE. HE'S YOURS...

THAT'S IT...

HUH?

What? Who's in love?

THAT'S LOVE, CHIHARU!!

NO HE DOESN'T!!

...HE THINKS I'M REALLY BORING, I JUST KNOW IT!

BUT, RISA...

She forgot "sewn up"!

WHAT'S SHE THINK HE IS— A PLANK, A FISH, OR A CAT?

WELL, WHATEVER IT IS, SHE'S PRETTY FIRED UP ABOUT IT.

What's she talking about?

I'LL GET HIM NAILED DOWN, ON ICE AND IN THE BAG! IT'S TOTALLY UNDER CONTROL!

JUST SIT BACK!

KTUNK

Huh?

SHHA

psst

THAT'S THE PLAN.

SO BASICALLY, ALL WE NEED IS FOR SUZUKI TO TELL TANAKA HE'S CRAZY ABOUT HER, RIGHT?

blah

SO LISTEN, I'LL MAKE SOME MOVES ON TANAKA TO PUT HIM IN A "NOW OR NEVER" FRAME OF MIND...

SURE IT'S FOR MYSELF, TOO!

AND YOU STAY BY HIM TO GIVE HIM A PUSH IF HE LOOKS LIKE HE NEEDS IT.

...IS SUCH A WUSS. BET HE GETS COLD FEET.

THE ONLY PROBLEM IS, SUZUKI...

I WANT TO HELP THOSE TWO GET TOGETHER, I REALLY DO!!

BUT EVEN MORE THAN THAT, IT'S FOR CHIHARU!!

blah

GOTCHA!

AND I GUESS THE REST IS UP TO SUZUKI.

HOW COME YOU DECIDED TO HELP ME OUT WITH THIS?

blah

HEY, OTANI...

I MEAN, WHAT DO YOU CARE IF I'M STILL HUNG UP ON SUZUKI OR NOT?

blah

blah

blah

HM?

...

IF YOU DON'T HURRY UP AND GET OVER SUZUKI, YOU WON'T FIND A BOYFRIEND.

AND IF YOU DON'T FIND A BOYFRIEND, EVERYBODY WILL KEEP SAYING YOU AND I ARE A COUPLE.

...

I CARE BECAUSE ...

UH-HUH?

OHH. SO THAT'S WHY.

...

...HEY ...

...

AND THAT IS THE *LAST* THING I NEED.

WHAT I DO IS NONE OF YOUR BUSINESS!

BUT FINE! YOU DON'T WANT ME TO HELP YOU OUT, I WON'T!

IN THIS CASE, IT'S *TOTALLY* MY BUSINESS!

IT'S THE LAST THING *I* NEED!!

WELL, SAME HERE, SHORTY!

UM... RISA?

OH, YEAH?! FINE!!

WHO NEEDS YOUR HELP, ANYWAY?! I CAN DEAL WITH THIS MYSELF!

SO HURRY UP AND DO SOMETHING ABOUT IT, YA DOPE!!

SHRIMP!

JUMBO-GAL!

...

HUH? BUT...

TAK

KLAK

AAA-ARGH! HE MAKES ME SO MAD!

SUZUKI-KUN.

I NEED TO TALK TO YOU.

HUH? BUT...

...OKAY...

IT'S NO BIG DEAL. LET'S GO AHEAD TO THE MOVIE THEATER.

WONDER WHAT'S THE MATTER...?

RISA??

BAM

UH...

NOT... THE WAY YOU MEAN ...

FORGET IT! LOOK, I KNOW YOU DO, OKAY?!

SUZUKI-KUN.

YOU REALLY LIKE CHIHARU A LOT, DON'T YOU?

SO WHAT'S THIS ABOUT ...?

...UMM ...

SO IF YOU WANNA GET TOGETHER WITH HER, GO TELL HER THAT!!

HUH?

RIGHT NOW!!

BUT ...

sorry...

BUT...

AAA-ARGH!

FINE, FORGET IT!

JUST GO FOR IT! YOU'RE REALLY BUGGING ME!!

OH, FOR CRYING OUT LOUD! STOP BEING SUCH A WUSS, WILL YOU?!

SEE?

WHO SAYS I NEED THAT STUPID ÔTANI'S HELP?

WHAAT?!

I'LL TELL CHIHARU FOR YOU, HOW'S THAT?!

THIS IS *MY* PROBLEM, SO I'LL TAKE CARE OF IT MYSELF!

HEY. FOUND THEM!

CHIHARU?

SO AFTER THAT, EVERYONE CALLED ME "KETCHUP." FOR YEARS. ALL THE WAY THROUGH SIXTH GRADE, I WAS "KETCHUP ŌTANI."

SO I'M TOTALLY CONKED OUT, RIGHT? AND WHEN THE TEACHER TAPS ME ON THE HEAD I GO, "MOM? I WANT SOME KETCHUP!"

HEE HEE HEE HEE! THAT IS SO FUNNY!

HEY, IT'S NO JOKE. THIS IS A VERY PAINFUL MEMORY, GIRL.

HEE HEE HEE HEE HEE!

CHI...

WHAT THE HECK ARE THEY TALKING ABOUT...?

...

NO WAY!

I GOT *TONS* OF STORIES LIKE THAT.

SURE.

YOU GOT ANY MORE?

TELL ME ANOTHER ONE!

WHAT'S THE MATTER?

...

...

tee hee

WONDER WHY IT IS....

...WHEN I'M WITH YOU, I'M TOTALLY NORMAL. I CAN TALK AND LAUGH AND EVERYTHING...

SO HOW COME I CAN'T DO THAT WHEN I'M WITH SUZUKI-KUN?

MAYBE...

TANAKA...

MAYBE...

I SHOULD HAVE A CRUSH ON SOMEBODY LIKE YOU, INSTEAD.

WHAT?

...

EXCUSE ME?! CHIHARU?!

HMMM.

I THINK YOU'RE LOOKING AT IT ALL WRONG.

HUH...?

...YEAH... BUT...

...THAT'S NOT...

I'M NOT A GUY, REMEMBER?

THE REASON YOU GET SO NERVOUS AROUND SUZUKI IS THAT HE'S A GUY TO YOU. YOU FEEL SELF-CONSCIOUS AROUND HIM CUZ YOU LIKE HIM.

THAT'S ALL IT IS. IT'S NORMAL!

...THAT YOU DON'T THINK OF ME AS A GUY.

YOU TOLD KOIZUMI AND NOBU BEFORE...

Tump

SO DON'T WORRY ABOUT IT! YOU'LL GET OVER IT!

ONCE YOU GET USED TO BEING AROUND HIM, YOU'LL BE ABLE TO TALK TO HIM JUST FINE!

...OKAY.

THANK YOU.

hanh

TELL HER WHAT...?

OH! NO...

NOT YET...

DID YOU DO IT?! DID YOU TELL HER?!

GOOD, CUZ I'M DOING IT!

GREEN!

OH, GOOD! I FOUND YOU!

NWAARGH!

SUZUKI-KUN...

HEY! GET YOUR BUTTS OVER HERE! THE MOVIE'S STARTING, DUDES!

hanh.

I WANNA DO IT...

...MYSELF...

hanh.

I'M TELLING TANAKA-SAN MYSELF. THAT I WANT TO GO OUT WITH HER.

SHUP

HUH?

TOK

TOK

TOK

TOK

WHAT TOOK YOU SO LO—

I...

I...

I...

I...

TANAKA-SAN!!

GULP

UH...

YES?!

SHUP

KA-BLONK

...yeah...?

I...'M SUZUKI.

WHAT THE HECK IS THAT DUDE SAYING?!

I THINK SHE ALREADY KNOWS THAT, SUZUKI-KUN!!

I REALLY LIKE YOU.

ERRR...

UMMM...

WILL YOU GO OUT WITH ME?

WELL...

...YES.

GOSH!

I FEEL SO MUCH BETTER NOW!

GOOD. THAT'S GREAT.

LIKE HOW?

...YOU ARE SUCH A DOPE, ŌTANI.

I MIGHT KILL YOU, DEPENDING ON THE ANSWER.

...

GET OUTTA HERE.

WHEN YOU WERE TALKING TO CHIHARU EARLIER...

...SHE MIGHT'VE FALLEN FOR YOU IF YOU'D SAID SOMETHING DIFFERENT.

HOW MANY TIMES DO I HAVE TO TELL YOU? I'M NOT A WISHY-WASHY LOSER LIKE YOU, OKAY?!

WHEN I BOW OUT, I STAY OUT. END OF STORY.

EXCUUUSE ME, MISTER MANLY-KINDA-GUY.

MAN, I CAN'T BELIEVE...

...THAT WE'RE GOING AROUND HELPING OTHER PEOPLE GET TOGETHER, LIKE WE GOT NOTHING BETTER TO DO.

OKAY, WHAT-EVER.

FINE, THEN.

YOU WANNA MAKE A BET?

WHOEVER GETS TOGETHER WITH SOMEONE FIRST WINS.

WHAT'LL YOU GIVE ME IF I WIN?

OKAY.

SO I'LL GIVE YOU WHATEVER YOU WANT IF *YOU* WIN.

WHATEVER YOU WANT.

GOOD. SO THAT'S SETTLED, THEN.

YOU'LL SEE. *I'M* GONNA WIN.

.....

WHY DOES THIS MAKE ME SO MAD?

OH, SHUT UP!

Whadja say?

GET AWAY FROM ME!

OOH, I'M DYING TO MESS IT UP...

WHAT'S WITH THE NEW LOOK, ANYWAY?

hedgehog sea urchin

I HAPPEN TO BE TOTALLY STYLIN' TODAY.

SHUT UP!

pff

WHAT'RE YOU TRYING TO LOOK LIKE, A HEDGEHOG? A SEA URCHIN?

Click THE MOUSE

CHAPTER 4

STARTING TODAY, I'M MISTER HOT. GIRLS ARE GONNA BE ALL OVER ME.

IF I GET TOGETHER WITH SOMEONE BEFORE YOU DO, YOU'LL GET ME WHATEVER I WANT, RIGHT? SO I WANT NEW BASKETBALL SHOES.

HUH? ME? WHAT FOR?

AND THEN YOU'RE GONNA BUY ME A NEW PAIR OF BASKETBALL SHOES!

VERGE

sneeek

...

WELL, *YOU* SEEM TO THINK A LITTLE LIPGLOSS IS ALL IT TAKES. LIKE, GET A CLUE.

OH, RIGHT. YOU JUST CHANGE YOUR HAIR AND GIRLS ARE GONNA BE ALL OVER YOU?

UAAAAAAAGH!

GOTCHA!!

I SHOULDN'T HAVE AGREED TO THAT BET SO FAST.

BZzzz

AND WHEN I FINALLY GET A CRUSH ON SOMEONE, HE GETS TOGETHER WITH A FRIEND OF MINE.

NOT THAT I'M PROUD OF IT, BUT I'VE NEVER HAD THE GUYS ALL OVER ME IN MY LIFE.

sure

OH.

OKAY!

NOBU! CHIHARU! LET'S GO HOME TOGETHER!

OF COURSE, I'VE NEVER EVEN ONCE HAD A BOYFRIEND.

This sure is a lot of fun...

Gee...

LOVEY

DOVEY

LOVEY

DOVEY

SO THERE IS NO WAY I'M GOING TO FIND MYSELF A BOYFRIEND, JUST LIKE THAT.

YOU CAN SAY *THAT* AGAIN.

I SWEAR I'M GONNA SUE YOU FOR REAL!

GO AHEAD. WHENEVER YOU WANT.

OOH, A "LOVE FORTUNE" MACHINE! HEY, DARLIN'! LET'S DO THIS!!

JEEZ, YOU HAVE ANY IDEA HOW LONG I SPENT ON MY HAIR THIS MORNING?

GROW UP! OH, SORRY, GUESS THAT ISN'T AN OPTION!

ARE YOU STILL GOING ON ABOUT YOUR HAIR?

LIMP

HEY, WHO ASKED *YOU* TO WALK HOME WITH US, ANYWAY?

I GOTTA GO BY NAKAO'S HOUSE FOR SOMETHING, ALL RIGHT?

143

HEY, CHIHARU AND SUZUKI! YOU WANNA TRY THIS?

WOW, 85 PERCENT! THAT'S REALLY GOOD!

THERE'S NO WAY THIS MUNCHKIN IS GOING TO FIND A GIRLFRIEND JUST LIKE THAT, EITHER.

HEY! STOP USING ME AS AN ARMREST!

GET HIM NEW BASKETBALL SHOES? NOT ON YOUR LIFE.

WELL, AT LEAST ŌTANI AND I ARE EVEN ON THAT COUNT.

HOW COMPATIBLE ARE YOU?

18%

GOTTA TRY HARDER!!

18... 18... EIGH... TEEN, HUH...

IT'S JUST A DUMB MACHINE, YOU GUYS!!

HA HA HA HA!

US?

MUTTR

18...

MUTTR

HA!

HEY, RISA, LET'S SEE WHAT IT SAYS FOR YOU AND ŌTANI! YOU KNOW, SINCE WE ALL DID IT?

tee hee! Just for fun?

NO WAY!!

WHAAAT?!

AS IF! WE AREN'T EXACTLY MADE FOR EACH OTHER.

psst

IT WON'T BE FUNNY.

WHAT IF IT SPITS OUT A NUMBER HIGHER THAN 18%?

BETCHA THIS MACHINE GIVES US THE FIRST ZERO IN ITS HISTORY!

CHEER UP, CHIHARU! COME WATCH THIS!!

18...

18...

VERGE

WHAT IS THIS, A SHAKE-DOWN?

SO SHUT UP AND GIMME SOME MONEY.

RIGHT?

GUESS YOU'RE RIGHT.

HEY!

KOIZUMI!

YOU REALLY PISS ME OFF...

INPUT ALL THE INFORMATION, THEN PUSH THE START BUTTON! ♥

Shut up

PUSH THE START BUTTON, HURRY!

NOW LET'S SEE WHAT YOUR CHANCES ARE! ♥

EXCUSE ME! DO YOU HAVE A FOOTSTOOL FOR LITTLE KIDS TO USE?

I'M TALL ENOUGH, YA DOPE!! Lay off'a me!

LOVE FORTUNE

This thing costs 400 yen?!

WHU MP

HOW COMPATIBLE ARE YOU?

100%

YOU'RE MADE FOR EACH OTHER!! ♥♥

NOW PRINTING

EXIT

VERGE

YOU'RE A PERFECT MATCH!! ♥

A HUNDRED PERCENT! ♥

RIGHT, YOU GUYS?!

I DON'T BELIEVE THIS! WHAT IS *WRONG* WITH THIS THING?!

HOW ARE WE 100 PERCENT COMPATIBLE, FER CRYIN' OUT LOUD?!

THIS THING IS OBVIOUSLY OUT OF WHACK!!

CHIHARU, COME ON!!

SO IF IT GAVE US 18, WE MUST BE REALLY ...

IT'S SET UP TO GIVE ONLY GOOD SCORES LIKE 100 AND 85, YOU CAN TELL...

100...

DO OM

I'M KINDA THIRSTY! WANNA STOP AND SIT DOWN SOME-PLACE?

Gee

uh-oh

mutter mutter mutter

18...

Everyone else gets high scores like 100 and 85, and we get 18...

HEY, SUZUKI. I THINK THIS IS YOUR CUE TO SAY SOME-THING.

OOPS.

FORTUNE-TELLING'S A LOT OF BALONEY, ANYWAY.

SAY THAT AGAIN, REAL LOUD, WILL YOU?

SO THAT THOSE TWO OVER THERE CAN HEAR YOU.

Bummin'

THAT MACHINE WAS TOTALLY SCREWY, I SWEAR.

HUH?

HEY, ÔTANI. WANNA GO SEE UMIBÔZU?

AS IF ÔTANI AND ME WOULD EVER BE 100 PERCENT COMPATIBLE.

A FRIEND OF MINE GOT A BUNCH OF TICKETS, AND THERE'S TWO LEFT.

OH, YEAH.

GIMME A BREAK.

UMI-BÔZU?!

FOR REAL?! I'M GOING!!

PWIK

MENU

RESTAURANT IKEBE

VERGE

I LOVED IT!

DOESN'T HE HAVE THE COOLEST VOICE?

YEAH, THE WAY IT'S...

YEAH, IT'S SO GREAT! DIDN'T YOU TOTALLY LOVE IT?!

YOU HEARD HIS LATEST ONE?!

I KNOW, HUH?! HE'S THE *BEST!*

VERGE

NO WAY! YOU LIKE HIM TOO?

ARE YOU KIDDING ME?!

HE TOTALLY ROCKS!!

I *LOVE* UMIBÔZU!!

OOPS

149

THE TWO OF US...?

...I DON'T KNOW...

IT'S NOT LIKE I'M A BIG FAN. I HARDLY EVEN KNOW HIS STUFF.

WHAAT?! BUT I THOUGHT YOU WERE GOING!

...WHY DON'T *YOU* TWO GO TO THE SHOW?

I THINK YOU GUYS REALLY ARE A PERFECT COUPLE.

HUH?

...

LEMME THINK ABOUT IT FOR A WHILE...

YOU KNOW WHAT I THINK? I THINK THAT MACHINE WAS RIGHT.

OKAY, SO WE BOTH HAPPEN TO BE NUTS ABOUT UMIBÔZU. SO WHAT?

NUTS? I'M SHOCKED! GIRLS SHOULD NOT USE SUCH SUGGESTIVE LANGUAGE!

NOT THE *MALE* KIND OF NUTS, OKAY?

WELL, IN AN UMIBÔZU-LOVING KINDA WAY, FOR ONE.

HOW?! IN WHAT WAY?!

UH, YES. COULD YOU HANG ON FOR JUST A MOMENT?

Ummm

ARE YOU READY TO ORDER?

Umm...

WELL, SAME HERE! I MEAN, LOOK WHO'S TALKING!

SEE? NO WAY I'D GET TOGETHER WITH SOMEONE THIS CRUDE.

chk chk chk

GOTTA TRY THIS.

NEW! FRUIT JUICE MIX

• To put you in a tropical mood...
Hawaiian Dancer

A NEW MENU ITEM?!

OOH!

151

I'LL HAVE THIS HAWAIIAN DANCER!

SEE?

They really are.

NO, WE ARE NOT!!

HERE YOU GO!

HEY, WHAT'RE THESE FLAGS FOR?

...BEING TOLD THAT ÔTANI AND I MAKE A PERFECT COUPLE...

...DOES NOT MAKE ME HAPPY.

blah

THANK YOU.

Sure thing.

KLATTER

OH, THOSE? WE ORDERED THEM BY MISTAKE.

YOU WANT TO STICK ONE IN YOUR OMELET, GO AHEAD.

It's on the house!

PSUP

REALLY? I THINK I WILL! YAY! ♡

BASICALLY...

HEY!

PSUP

HMM?

IT'S LIKE A KIDDIE LUNCH. SO CUTE! ♡

IT ONLY GETS IN THE WAY.

tee hee

I BET YOU'RE THE ONLY IDIOT WHO TOOK ONE.

blah

blah

blah

blah

YEAH, BUT YOU GUYS GET ALONG REALLY WELL.

LISTEN, RISA...

HERE'S ANOTHER IDIOT WHO TOOK ONE.

HAVING THE SAME TASTES AND STUFF COUNTS FOR A LOT, YOU KNOW?

Can't have.

WELL, YEAH, CUZ WE'RE IN LOVE. ♡

Like which movies to see.

LIKE, ME AND NAKAO GET IN A LOT OF FIGHTS BECAUSE WE DON'T.

FIRST OF ALL, HE'S GOTTA BE TALLER THAN ME!

SUCH AS?

HAVING THE SAME TASTES DOESN'T COUNT FOR *ANYTHING* IF YOU'RE NOT IN LOVE!

ZWUP

This flag, big deal!!

AND GOOD-LOOKING! AND EASY-GOING! AND REALLY NICE! AND—LET'S SEE, WHAT ELSE...

HE DOESN'T EXIST.

AND ANYHOW, I HAPPEN TO HAVE TASTES IN GUYS, TOO!

4.

Oops!! We're almost at the end. Thank you for reading this far. I hope I get to meet you again in Vol. 2. And thank you to everybody who sends me letters! I read every single one. But I can't answer them all, which is causing this scrupulous artist chronic stomach pains. So I'd like to take these feelings of gratitude and repay you through my manga!! And I'm trying to do that. I really am... but is it showing...?

Well, see you again! ✷
Aya
February 2002

✦ Special Thanks ✦
Rumiko Sawada
Nana Ikebe
Aki Nakahara

and you ♥

FINE, WELL, ALL I *REALLY* CARE ABOUT IS IF HE'S TALLER THAN ME, OKAY?!

WHY'RE YOU SO DESPERATE?

YOU KNOW ANYBODY?!

I MEAN, ŌTANI'S REALLY POPULAR.

WHAT'S THAT SUPPOSED TO MEAN?

BECAUSE I MADE A BET WITH ŌTANI, TO SEE WHO GETS TOGETHER WITH SOMEONE FIRST.

WELL, YOU'RE IN TROUBLE, RISA. HE'S GONNA WIN FOR SURE!

YOU DID?!

I'm done 18... See you later 18...

ÔTANI'S POPULAR?

THAT LITTLE SHRIMP?

BUT HE *CAN'T* BE.

KTUNK

...SURELY YOU JEST.

I'M ABSOLUTELY SERIOUS.

OVER THERE. SEE THEM?

LET'S SEE. WHERE ARE THEY?

FWEE

BWOMP

I'm going back to the classroom 18...

wobble

YEAH. SHE'S TRAUMATIZED BY THAT 18 PERCENT.

WE GOTTA DO SOMETHING TO GET HER OUT OF THAT.

I THINK THEY'RE SECOND- OR THIRD-YEAR GIRLS.

ANYWAY, THEY'RE ALWAYS WATCHING ÔTANI AND SQUEALING.

ARE YOU SERIOUS?

BWOMP

BWOMP

REALLY? OH, YEAH.

OH, LOOK. ÔTANI-KUN'S GETTING YELLED AT BY THE COACH AGAIN.

HE IS SO *CUTE!* ♡

SEE?

THUNK

UH!

CUTE ?!

OF COURSE! LITTLE GUYS HAVE THE "CUTE" CARD TO PLAY!!

HOW TOTALLY UNFAIR!!

ROLL

OHHH, FROM OUR SISTER! WELL, AREN'T WE ADORABLE! ♡

THESE? I BORROWED 'EM FROM MY SIS CUZ...

PINNING OUR HAIR TO THE SIDES LIKE A CUTE LIDDLE GIRL! ♡

ARE WE UPPING OUR CUTESY-NESS WITH THOSE SWEET LIDDLE FLOWER PINS?

OH-HO!

HUH?

WHAT'S WITH THAT CRAB-UGLY LOOK ON YOUR FACE...?

SO WE'RE EVEN! BUT I'M NOT LOSING TO YOU, YOU HEAR ME?!

WATCH IT! YOU'RE STARTING TO PISS ME OFF.

WHAT ?!

I'M GOING TO WIN OUR BET AND MAKE YOU BUY ME A WHOLE PILE OF NEW GAMES, SO THERE!!

DARN HIM. IT'S JUST SO UNFAIR...

WHAT'S EATING *HER* ALL OF A SUDDEN?

Might've known it would be games.

DA DA DA DA DA DA DA DA

hyelp

...

DAZE

DUM
DA DI
DA DUM
DA

BEING ALL POPULAR, ALL BY HIMSELF...

DUM
DA DI
DA
DUM
DA

THAK

THAK

BIP

I'M SICK OF THAT JERK! I'M BREAKING UP WITH HIM!!

CUT IT OUT?

Gee, sorry.

EXCUSE ME?

EXCUSE ME?

ER, NO, AGENT 007 IS NOT IN AT THE...

YERRRS, HER MAJESTY'S SECRET SERVICE.

WOULD YOU LIKE THAT SHAKEN, MADAM, OR STIRRED?

TITANIC PITANIC

A TITLE CATERING HOMAGE HAVING THE BIGGEST BOOBS YOU EVER SAW!

SALE

OH...SO WHAT'S THE BIG DEAL?

That's pretty normal.

...WHOA, NOBU. WHAT'S GOING ON?

HE *BOUGHT* IT! USED, BUT STILL! HE ACTUALLY *OWNS* IT!

IT'S A BIG DEAL TO ME!! I MEAN, IT ISN'T EVEN A RENTAL!

I FOUND A PORNO VIDEO STASHED IN HIS ROOM!!

YOU WON'T BELIEVE THIS!!

HEH?

WELL, I'M FOOLING AROUND ON HIM!!

SORRY... I CAN'T OFFER AN OPINION ON THAT.

I MEAN TO SAY, AREN'T I ENOUGH?!

WHEN HE'S GOT *ME* AS HIS GIRL-FRIEND!!

...A KARAOKE NIGHT...?

YOU MIGHT MEET THE GUY OF YOUR DREAMS, RISA!

I GOT A FRIEND OF MINE TO SET UP A KARAOKE NIGHT WITH A BUNCH OF GUYS. WHY DON'T YOU COME TOO?!

TOTALLY!

YOU WANNA GO?

THE GUY OF MY DREAMS ...

...MAKE THAT SHRIMP CRY UNCLE!!

WHO SAYS I HAVE TO LOSE THE BET JUST BECAUSE A FEW GIRLS THINK ÔTANI'S CUTE?

I'M GONNA GO ALL OUT TONIGHT, FIND ME A GORGEOUS HUNK, AND...

unqqq   qqlrqh

SAME HERE.

EXCEPT IT WAS MY FRIEND FROM MIDDLE SCHOOL.

THEY DIDN'T HAVE ENOUGH PEOPLE, SO NOBU ASKED ME TO COME!

WHAT ON EARTH ARE *YOU* DOING HERE?!

I WAS JUST ABOUT TO ASK YOU THE SAME QUESTION!

...HOW...

ha ha ha

YEAH, I WANT A REBATE!!

YOU WANT A REBATE?! *YOU* WANT A REBATE?!

HOW COME ...?

HEYYY...

NO, *I* WANT A REBATE!!

HEY, GIMME A REBATE FOR *HER*, DUDE. WHAT A RIP-OFF!

JEEZ! HERE I COME THINKING I MIGHT MEET A HOT CHICK OR TWO, AND ONE OF THEM'S *YOU?*

AND WE'RE ALL FRIENDS OF ÔTANI'S FRIEND.

HI! NICE TO MEETCHA! I'M A FRIEND OF ÔTANI'S.

DON'T TELL ME YOU TWO ALREADY KNOW EACH OTHER?

Huh?

YEAH.

GUINEA PIG

CAT

MONKEY

DOG

THE PET SHOP BOYS ...

OH. HELLO...

HEEEEERE YOU GO, RISA!

OH, WHO CARES WHAT THEY LOOK LIKE?!

PERSONALITY IS WHAT REALLY COUNTS!

WHAT'S SHE MUTTERING LIKE SOME BAG LADY?

MUTTER

WELL, BETTER PETS THAN FARM ANIMALS...

OR MARINE PRODUCTS, LIKE SHRIMP.

MUTTER

MUTTER

COME ON, RISA, WE'RE GOING.

Ha ha ha...

I SAY, YOOOO! YOOOO! YO! YO! YO! YO!

UH-HUH ...

HEYYYY, WHASS UP?! WE'RE HERE TO PARTY, RIGHT?! CHEER UP, GIRL!

...THANKS...

...FIVE SEVEN...

...KNEW IT...

SO HEY, BY THE WAY... WHAT'S YOUR HEIGHT?

ZWOZ

WOW, THAT'S REALLY TALL!

figures...

OH MY GOD...

Ha ha ha ha ha ha ha ha.

Just kidding!

IF YOU'RE ALREADY THAT TALL NOW, BET YOU'LL BE ABOUT NINE FEET BY THE TIME YOU GRADUATE!

GET ME OUT OF HERE... THIS GUY IS SUCH A DORK...

ha ha ha ha ha

NINE FEET, *HA HA!* I'M A RIOT, HUH? MY FRIENDS ALL CALL ME THE JOKER!

Ha ha ha. Yeah, right. I hope not...

URRR-RRGH...

MONTEREY JACK!

YO!

CLOSER TOGETHER, YOU GUYS!

OKAY, SAY CHEESE!

One more!

KA-CHAK

KLIK

JUST STEPPING OUTSIDE FOR SOME FRESH AIR.

HEY, ŌTANI-KUN? WHERE ARE YOU GOING?

WHAAT?

167

PFFF

KREE

KLAK

DYING

PHO

Whaddaya mean, your song? Like, you wrote it?

Yup

hyargh

I think I just met the guy of my nightmares...

Nobu... Help...

da-di-daaa

WHAT'S SO DARN FUNNY?!

WHO PUT THIS ONE ON?

HEY, THAT'S MY SONG!

168

URGH...

THAT'S WHY I'M SAYING THAT HAVING THE SAME TASTES AND STUFF REALLY MATTERS.

HOW MANY GUYS ARE YOU GONNA MEET WHO'RE 100 PERCENT COMPATIBLE WITH YOU?

I MEAN, HE THINKS HE'S FUNNY AND I DON'T... LIKE, WE JUST DON'T CLICK...

I KNOW, BUT HE'S SUCH A GIANT PAIN.

I THOUGHT ALL YOU REALLY CARED ABOUT WAS IF HE WAS TALLER THAN YOU.

...HMMM...

I REALLY THINK ÔTANI'S THE BEST GUY FOR YOU, RISA. I'M TOTALLY SERIOUS.

HEY THERE.

...UH ...NO.

HUH?

YEAH.

YOU KNOW THAT GUY ÔTANI, RIGHT? HE'S A FRIEND OF YOURS?

OH, GOOD! THAT'S WHAT WE WERE HOPING.

HE DOESN'T HAVE A GIRLFRIEND, DOES HE? IF HE'S HERE TONIGHT.

YOU THINK HE'S CUTE?

...UM...

DON'T... ...TELL ME...

...OH MY GOD.

HE'S TOTALLY ADORABLE! ♡

SQUEAL

SQUEAL

I REALLY MIGHT END UP BUYING HIM THOSE BASKET- BALL SHOES...

KA-CHAK

YOUR SEAT'S ON THE OTHER SIDE.

WHY'RE YOU HERE...?

YOU WANT THAT DUDE WHO DRIVES YOU CRAZY TO COME SIT BESIDE YOU AGAIN?

WONDER HOW MUCH A PAIR OF THOSE THINGS COSTS...

...IT DID...?

YOU LOOKED LIKE YOU WERE DYING A SLOW AND PAINFUL DEATH.

THANKS A LOT.

...WHAT?

YOUR FACE HAD "GET ME OUTTA HERE" WRITTEN ALL OVER IT.

ALL THE GIRLS HERE.

THEY THINK YOU'RE ADORABLE.

NO WAY...

THE EVIL EYE? FROM WHO?

BUT IF YOU DON'T GO BACK TO YOUR SEAT, I'M GONNA GET THE EVIL EYE.

I WANNA BE GOOD-LOOKING! OR HOT! OR HUNKY! OKAY?

WHAT'S WRONG WITH IT?

...HUH?

EVERY-THING'S WRONG WITH IT!

NO, YOU SAID THEY THINK I'M ADOR-ABLE!

WHAT'S YOUR PROBLEM? I JUST TOLD YOU THE GIRLS ARE TOTALLY INTO YOU.

CUTE IS BAD ENOUGH, BUT WHAT KINDA GUY WANTS TO BE ADOR-ABLE?

...AND...

...GOSH. WHO KNEW?

JUST DO ME A FAVOR AND LET ME STAY HERE, WILL YA?

I swear my head's still spinning.

THE REASON I HAD TO STEP OUTSIDE WAS, THEY GOT ON SO MUCH PERFUME IT'S MAKING ME FEEL SICK.

PFFFF

WHAT'S SO DARN FUNNY?!

OMIGOD, THIS IS—!!

UMIBŌZU?! BUT HOW?!

NO WAY!

hee hee

JEEZ.

WE ARE BOTH TOTALLY HOPELESS AT THIS!

BUT WHY DO THEY EVEN HAVE UMIBŌZU IN THE FIRST PLACE?!

I PUT IT ON.

OMIGOD!! I DON'T BELIEVE IT! I'M SINGING THIS WITH YOU!!

I KNOW, YOU'D THINK HE'S WAY TOO OBSCURE FOR KARAOKE, RIGHT?!

GRIN

TOTALLY INTO IT

WOOO WEEE

WOOO WEEE

WOOO WEEE

WOOO WEEE

WANOWEWWOO

WANOOO

HEY!!

COOL, SO YOU COME IN AT THE REFRAIN, OKAY?!

okay

YOU GOT IT! I AM SO ON IT!

HERE WE GO!

heh heh

kitchee koo

Okay.

Can I have your cell phone number?

Really?

I'll walk you home.

...Bye, every-body...

BYE, YOU GUYS! KONDO-KUN HERE'S GONNA WALK ME HOME.

OH!

BUT I DID HAVE FUN WHEN UMIBÔZU CAME ON!

OMIGOD, I SWEAR, THAT FELT SO GOOD!

...ÔTANI ISN'T SO BAD-LOOKING. HE'S ACTUALLY PRETTY CUTE.

I KNOW, HUH?! ME TOO!

ME EITHER, MAN! I ALMOST DIED WHEN I SAW IT THERE!

I CAN'T BELIEVE YOU FOUND THAT, ÔTANI!

PLUS WE'RE BOTH INTO ALL THE SAME THINGS...

...AND WE CAN TALK ABOUT ALL KINDS OF STUFF...

OH MY GOSH, I ALMOST HAD A HEART ATTACK!!

I *REALLY* WANTED TO TELL YOU, LIKE, THAT MOMENT, BUT I DECIDED IT'D BE BETTER TO SURPRISE YOU BY HAVING IT SUDDENLY COME ON, SO I KEPT QUIET ABOUT IT.

I KNEW YOU WOULD!

WHAT IT SAID ABOUT US BEING 100 PERCENT COMPATIBLE.

...

THAT MACHINE.

I'M STARTING TO THINK MAYBE IT WAS RIGHT.

HEH?

...ISN'T THAT THE BIGGEST PROBLEM, THOUGH?

APART FROM OUR HEIGHTS.

IT'S NOT LIKE WE'RE GONNA START GOING OUT OR ANYTHING.

PROBLEM? FOR WHAT?

...OH, YEAH.

...SEE?

...HEY, KOIZUMI.

HM?

BEING 100 PERCENT COMPATIBLE DOESN'T COUNT FOR ANYTHING IF YOU AREN'T IN LOVE.

...YOU WANNA GO SEE THAT UMIBÔZU SHOW TOGETHER? YOU KNOW, JUST CUZ.

ALL IT MEANS IS WE BOTH GET REALLY EXCITED SINGING UMIBÔZU SONGS TOGETHER.

YEAH!

WELL, AT LEAST IT LOOKS LIKE I WON'T HAVE TO BUY HIM THOSE BASKETBALL SHOES RIGHT AWAY.

《to be continued》

glossary

Page 9, panel 6: All Hanshin-Kyojin
All Hanshin-Kyojin are a *manzai* duo from the late '70s-early '80s and still perform today. Mainzai are two-person stand-up comedy acts with one person acting as the *boke* (fool) and the other as the *tsukkomi* (who constantly castigates the *boke* for his foolishness). *Kyojin* is Japanese for "giant," and is used as a nickname for the Tokyo-based Yomiuri Giants. The Kansai-based Hanshin Tigers are called "Hanshin" rather than "the Tigers." These two baseball teams are in constant rivalry—at least in Kansai people's minds—even though the Tigers tend to be at the bottom of the league standings and the Giants at the top. The manzai duo All Hanshin-Kyojin consists of a shrimp (Hanshin) and a giant (Kyojin).

Page 58, panel 5: Nori-tsukkomi
A type of comedy delivery when you pretend to go along with the set-up, and then turn around and call the other person on it, like Ôtani does in this scene.

Page 78, panel 1: Yukata
Summer kimono, usually made of brightly colored cotton. The yukata originated as a bathrobe in the Heian period, and the word comes from *yu* (bath) and *katabira* (underclothes). Today, yukata are often worn during summer festivals and fireworks displays or at traditional Japanese inns.

Page 148, panel 6: Umibôzu
The name of Risa and Ôtani's favorite group means "sea goblin."

Page 162, panel 5: Karaoke night
This is called *gôkon* in Japanese and is a party for meeting people, like a big group date with no commitment. Usually, gôkan are made up of 10-12 people, like the one here.

Page 165, panel 6: The Pet Shop Boys
The original Japanese references the folk tale "Momotaro," or Peach Boy, who is accompanied on his adventure by a pheasant, a monkey, and a dog.

Ever since my debut I've been using the same mechanical pencil that a friend gave me when I landed my first job. But the other day it suddenly disappeared. I went to the store hoping to find the same model, but they didn't have it, so I bought a whole bunch of different ones and am now auditioning them.
But...it's gotta be **that** one!
Waaaah!!

Aya Nakahara won the 2003 Shogakukan manga award for her breakthrough hit *Love★Com*, which was made into a major motion picture and a PS2 game in 2006. She debuted with *Haru to Kuuki Nichiyo-bi* in 1995, and her other works include *HANADA* and *Himitsu Kichi*.

LOVE★COM VOL 1
The Shojo Beat Manga Edition

STORY AND ART BY
AYA NAKAHARA

Translation & English Adaptation/Pookie Rolf
Touch-up Art & Lettering/Gia Cam Luc
Design/Amy Martin
Editor/Pancha Diaz

Editor in Chief, Books/Alvin Lu
Editor in Chief, Magazines/Marc Weidenbaum
VP of Publishing Licensing/Rika Inouye
VP of Sales/Gonzalo Ferreyra
Sr. VP of Marketing/Liza Coppola
Publisher/Hyoe Narita

Published by VIZ Media, LLC
P.O. Box 77010
San Francisco, CA 94107

Shojo Beat Manga Edition
10 9 8 7 6 5 4 3 2
First printing, July 2007
Second printing, December 2007

PARENTAL ADVISORY
LOVE★COM is rated T for Teen and is
recommended for ages 13 and up.
ratings.viz.com

store.viz.com

Tell us what you think about Shojo Beat Manga!

surv

lab

asurvey

...help us make our
...fferings

...a Tanemura/SHUEISHA Inc.
...ASE/Shogakukan Inc.
...AKUSENSHA, Inc.

SO-AEH-995